The Golden Age

The Golden Age

by
KENNETH GRAHAME

WORDSWORTH CLASSICS

This edition published 1995 by Wordsworth Editions Ltd,
Cumberland House, Crib Street, Ware, Hertfordshire SG12 9ET.

ISBN 1-85326-152-1

Printed and bound in Denmark by Nørhaven.

The paper in this book is produced from pure wood
pulp, without the use of chlorine or any other substance
harmful to the environment. The energy used in its
production consists almost entirely of hydroelectricity
and heat generated from waste materials, thereby
conserving fossil fuels and contributing little to the
greenhouse effect.

CONTENTS

PROLOGUE: THE OLYMPIANS

LOOKING back to those days of old, ere the gate shut to behind me, I can see now that to children with a proper equipment of parents these things would have worn a different aspect. But to those whose nearest were aunts and uncles, a special attitude of mind may be allowed. They treated us, indeed, with kindness enough as to the needs of the flesh, but after that with indifference (an indifference, as I recognise, the result of a certain stupidity), and therewith the commonplace conviction that your child is merely animal. At a very early age I remember realising in a quite impersonal and kindly way the existence of that stupidity, and its tremendous influence in the world; while there grew up in me, as in the parallel case of Caliban upon Setebos, a vague sense of a ruling power, wilful, and freakish, and prone to the practice of vagaries—'just choosing so':

as, for instance, the giving of authority over us
to these hopeless and incapable creatures, when
it might far more reasonably have been given
to ourselves over them.   These elders, our
betters by a trick of chance, commanded no
respect, but only a certain blend of envy—of
their good luck—and pity—for their inability
to make use of it.   Indeed, it was one of the
most hopeless features in their character (when
we troubled ourselves to waste a thought on
them : which wasn't often) that, having absolute
licence to indulge in the pleasures of life, they
could get no good of it.   They might dabble in
the pond all day, hunt the chickens, climb trees
in the most uncompromising Sunday clothes ;
they were free to issue forth and buy gunpowder in the full eye of the sun—free to fire
cannons and explode mines on the lawn : yet
they never did any one of these things.   No
irresistible Energy haled them to church o'
Sundays ; yet they went there regularly of their
own accord, though they betrayed no greater
delight in the experience than ourselves.

On the whole, the existence of these Olympians seemed to be entirely void of interests,
even as their movements were confined and

slow, and their habits stereotyped and senseless.
To anything but appearances they were blind.
For them the orchard (a place elf-haunted,
wonderful!) simply produced so many apples
and cherries: or it didn't—when the failures of
Nature were not infrequently ascribed to us.
They never set foot within fir-wood or hazel-
copse, nor dreamt of the marvels hid therein.
The mysterious sources, sources as of old Nile,
that fed the duck-pond had no magic for them.
They were unaware of Indians, nor recked they
anything of bisons or of pirates (with pistols!),
though the whole place swarmed with such
portents. They cared not to explore for
robbers' caves, nor dig for hidden treasure.
Perhaps, indeed, it was one of their best qualities that they spent the greater part of their
time stuffily indoors.

To be sure there was an exception in the
curate, who would receive, unblenching, the
information that the meadow beyond the
orchard was a prairie studded with herds of
buffalo, which it was our delight, moccasined
and tomahawked, to ride down with those
whoops that announce the scenting of blood.
He neither laughed nor sneered, as the

Olympians would have done; but, possessed
of a serious idiosyncrasy, he would contribute
such lots of valuable suggestion as to the
pursuit of this particular sort of big game that,
as it seemed to us, his mature age and eminent
position could scarce have been attained without a practical knowledge of the creature in its
native lair.   Then, too, he was always ready to
constitute himself a hostile army or a band of
marauding Indians on the shortest possible
notice: in brief, a distinctly able man, with
talents, so far as we could judge, immensely
above the majority.   I trust he is a bishop by
this time.   He had all the necessary qualifications, as we knew.

These strange folk had visitors sometimes—
stiff and colourless Olympians like themselves,
equally without vital interests and intelligent
pursuits : emerging out of the clouds, and
passing away again to drag on an aimless
existence somewhere beyond our ken.   Then
brute force was pitilessly applied.   We were
captured, washed, and forced into clean collars :
silently submitting as was our wont, with more
contempt than anger.   Anon, with unctuous
hair and faces stiffened in a conventional grin,

we sat and listened to the usual platitudes. How could reasonable people spend their precious time so? That was ever our wonder as we bounded forth at last: to the old clay-pit to make pots, or to hunt bears among the hazels.

It was perennial matter for amazement how these Olympians would talk over our heads— during meals, for instance—of this or the other social or political inanity, under the delusion that these pale phantasms of reality were among the importances of life. We *illuminati*, eating silently, our heads full of plans and conspiracies, could have told them what real life was. We had just left it outside, and were all on fire to get back to it. Of course we didn't waste the revelation on them: the futility of imparting our ideas had long been demon-strated. One in thought and purpose, linked by the necessity of combating one hostile fate, a power antagonistic ever—a power we lived to evade—we had no confidants save ourselves. This strange anæmic order of beings was further removed from us, in fact, than the kindly beasts who shared our natural existence in the sun. The estrangement was fortified by an abiding

sense of injustice, arising from the refusal of the
Olympians ever to defend, to retract, to admit
themselves in the wrong, or to accept similar
concessions on our part. For instance, when I
flung the cat out of an upper window (though I
did it from no ill-feeling, and it didn't hurt the
cat), I was ready, after a moment's reflection,
to own I was wrong, as a gentleman should.
But was the matter allowed to end there? I
trow not. Again, when Harold was locked up
in his room all day, for assault and battery
upon a neighbour's pig—an action he would
have scorned: being indeed on the friendliest
terms with the porker in question—there was
no handsome expression of regret on the discovery of the real culprit. What Harold had
felt was not so much the imprisonment—
indeed, he had very soon escaped by the
window, with assistance from his allies, and
had only gone back in time for his release—
as the Olympian habit. A word would have
set all right; but of course that word was
never spoken.

Well! The Olympians are all past and
gone. Somehow the sun does not seem to
shine so brightly as it used; the trackless

meadows of old time have shrunk and dwindled away to a few poor acres. A saddening doubt, a dull suspicion, creeps over me. *Et in Arcadia ego*—I certainly did once inhabit Arcady. Can it be that I also have become an Olympian?

A HOLIDAY

THE masterful wind was up and out, shouting and chasing, the lord of the morning. Poplars swayed and tossed with a roaring swish; dead leaves sprang aloft, and whirled into space; and all the clear-swept heaven seemed to thrill with sound like a great harp. It was one of the first awakenings of the year. The earth stretched herself, smiling in her sleep; and everything leapt and pulsed to the stir of the giant's movement. With us it was a whole holiday; the occasion a birthday—it matters not whose. Some one of us had had presents, and pretty conventional speeches, and had glowed with that sense of heroism which is no less sweet that nothing has been done to deserve it. But the holiday was for all, the rapture of awakening Nature for all, the various outdoor joys of puddles and sun and hedge-breaking for all. Colt-like I ran through the

meadows, frisking happy heels in the face of
Nature laughing responsive. Above, the sky
was bluest of the blue ; wide pools left by the
winter's floods flashed the colour back, true and
brilliant ; and the soft air thrilled with the
germinating touch that seems to kindle something in my own small person as well as in
the rash primrose already lurking in sheltered
haunts. Out into the brimming sun-bathed
world I sped, free of lessons, free of discipline
and correction, for one day at least. My legs
ran of themselves, and though I heard my
name called faint and shrill behind, there was
no stopping for me. It was only Harold, I concluded, and his legs, though shorter than mine,
were good for a longer spurt than this. Then
I heard it called again, but this time more
faintly, with a pathetic break in the middle ;
and I pulled up short, recognising Charlotte's
plaintive note.

She panted up anon, and dropped on the
turf beside me. Neither had any desire for talk ;
the glow and the glory of existing on this perfect
morning were satisfaction full and sufficient.

'Where's Harold?' I asked presently.

'Oh, he's just playin' muffin-man, as usual,'

said Charlotte with petulance. 'Fancy wanting to be a muffin-man on a whole holiday!'

It was a strange craze, certainly; but Harold,
who invented his own games and played them
without assistance, always stuck staunchly to
a new fad, till he had worn it quite out. Just
at present he was a muffin-man, and day and
night he went through passages and up and
down staircases, ringing a noiseless bell and
offering phantom muffins to invisible wayfarers.
It sounds a poor sort of sport; and yet—to
pass along busy streets of your own building,
for ever ringing an imaginary bell and offering
airy muffins of your own make to a bustling
thronging crowd of your own creation—there
were points about the game, it cannot be
denied, though it seemed scarce in harmony
with this radiant wind-swept morning!

'And Edward, where is he?' I questioned
again.

'He's coming along by the road,' said Charlotte. 'He'll be crouching in the ditch when
we get there, and he's going to be a grizzly
bear and spring out on us, only you mustn't
say I told you, 'cos it's to be a surprise.'

'All right,' I said magnanimously. 'Come

on and let's be surprised.' But I could not
help feeling that on this day of days even a
grizzly felt misplaced and common.

Sure enough an undeniable bear sprang out
on us as we dropped into the road; then
ensued shrieks, growlings, revolver-shots, and
unrecorded heroisms, till Edward condescended
at last to roll over and die, bulking large and
grim, an unmitigated grizzly. It was an understood thing, that whoever took upon himself
to be a bear must eventually die, sooner or
later, even if he were the eldest born; else,
life would have been all strife and carnage,
and the Age of Acorns have displaced our hard-
won civilisation. This little affair concluded
with satisfaction to all parties concerned, we
rambled along the road, picking up the defaulting Harold by the way, muffinless now and in
his right and social mind.

'What would you do?' asked Charlotte
presently — the book of the moment always
dominating her thoughts until it was sucked
dry and cast aside,—'What would you do if
you saw two lions in the road, one on each
side, and you didn't know if they was loose
or if they was chained up?'

'Do?' shouted Edward valiantly, 'I should —I should—I should—' His boastful accents died away into a mumble: 'Dunno what I should do.'

'Shouldn't do anything,' I observed after consideration; and, really, it would be difficult to arrive at a wiser conclusion.

'If it came to *doing*,' remarked Harold reflectively, 'the lions would do all the doing there was to do, wouldn't they?'

'But if they was *good* lions,' rejoined Charlotte, 'they would do as they would be done by.'

'Ah, but how are you to know a good lion from a bad one?' said Edward. 'The books don't tell you at all, and the lions ain't marked any different.'

'Why, there aren't any good lions,' said Harold hastily.

'O yes, there are, heaps and heaps,' contradicted Edward. 'Nearly all the lions in the story-books are good lions. There was Androcles' lion, and St. Jerome's lion, and— and—and the Lion and the Unicorn——'

'He beat the Unicorn,' observed Harold dubiously, 'all round the town.'

'That *proves* he was a good lion,' cried Edward triumphantly. 'But the question is, how are you to tell 'em when you see 'em?'

'*I* should ask Martha,' said Harold of the simple creed.

Edward snorted contemptuously, then turned to Charlotte. 'Look here,' he said; 'let's play at lions, anyhow, and I'll run on to that corner and be a lion,—I'll be two lions, one on each side of the road,—and you'll come along, and you won't know whether I'm chained up or not, and that'll be the fun!'

'No, thank you,' said Charlotte firmly; 'you'll be chained up till I'm quite close to you, and then you'll be loose, and you'll tear me in pieces, and make my frock all dirty, and p'raps you'll hurt me as well. *I* know your lions!'

'No, I won't, I swear I won't,' protested Edward. 'I'll be quite a new lion this time —something you can't even imagine.' And he raced off to his post. Charlotte hesitated— then she went timidly on, at each step growing less Charlotte, the mummer of a minute, and more the anxious Pilgrim of all time. The lion's wrath waxed terrible at her approach;

his roaring filled the startled air. I waited
until they were both thoroughly absorbed, and
then I slipped through the hedge out of the
trodden highway, into the vacant meadow
spaces. It was not that I was unsociable, nor
that I knew Edward's lions to the point of
satiety; but the passion and the call of the
divine morning were high in my blood. Earth
to earth! That was the frank note, the joyous
summons of the day; and they could not but
jar and seem artificial, these human discussions
and pretences, when boon nature, reticent no
more, was singing that full-throated song of
hers that thrills and claims control of every
fibre. The air was wine, the moist earth-smell
wine, the lark's song, the wafts from the cow-
shed at top of the field, the pant and smoke
of a distant train — all were wine—or song,
was it? or odour, this unity they all blent into?
I had no words then to describe it, that earth-
effluence of which I was so conscious; nor,
indeed, have I found words since. I ran sideways, shouting; I dug glad heels into the
squelching soil; I splashed diamond showers
from puddles with a stick; I hurled clods sky-
wards at random, and presently I somehow

found myself singing. The words were mere nonsense—irresponsible babble; the tune was an improvisation, a weary, unrhythmic thing of rise and fall: and yet it seemed to me a genuine utterance, and just at that moment the one thing fitting and right and perfect. Humanity would have rejected it with scorn. Nature, everywhere singing in the same key, recognised and accepted it without a flicker of dissent.

All the time the hearty wind was calling to me companionably from where he swung and bellowed in the tree-tops. 'Take me for guide to-day,' he seemed to plead. 'Other holidays you have tramped it in the track of the stolid, unswerving sun; a belated truant, you have dragged a weary foot homeward with only a pale, expressionless moon for company. To-day why not I, the trickster, the hypocrite? I who whip round corners and bluster, relapse and evade, then rally and pursue! I can lead you the best and rarest dance of any; for I am the strong capricious one, the lord of mis-rule, and I alone am irresponsible and un-principled, and obey no law.' And for me, I was ready enough to fall in with the fellow's humour; was not this a whole holiday? So we sheered off together, arm-in-arm, so to speak; and with fullest confidence I took the jigging, thwartwise course my chainless pilot laid for me.

A whimsical comrade I found him, ere he had done with me. Was it in jest, or with some serious purpose of his own, that he brought me plump upon a pair of lovers, silent, face to face o'er a discreet unwinking stile? As a rule this sort of thing struck me as the most pitiful tomfoolery. Two calves rubbing noses through a gate were natural and right and within the order of things; but that human beings, with salient interests and active pursuits beckoning them on from every side, could thus—! Well, it was a thing to hurry past, shamed of face, and think on no more. But this morning everything I met seemed to be accounted for and set in tune by that same magical touch in the air; and it was with a certain surprise that I found myself regarding these fatuous ones with kindliness instead of contempt, as I rambled by, unheeded of them. There was indeed some reconciling influence abroad, which could bring the like antics into

harmony with bud and growth and the frolic
air.

A puff on the right cheek from my wilful
companion sent me off at a fresh angle, and
presently I came in sight of the village church,
sitting solitary within its circle of elms. From
forth the vestry window projected two small
legs, gyrating, hungry for foothold, with larceny
—not to say sacrilege—in their every wriggle:
a godless sight for a supporter of the Establishment. Though the rest was hidden, I knew the
legs well enough; they were usually attached
to the body of Bill Saunders, the peerless bad
boy of the village. Bill's coveted booty, too,
I could easily guess at that; it came from the
Vicar's store of biscuits, kept (as I knew) in
a cupboard along with his official trappings.
For a moment I hesitated; then I passed on
my way. I protest I was not on Bill's side;
but then, neither was I on the Vicar's, and
there was something in this immoral morning
which seemed to say that perhaps, after all,
Bill had as much right to the biscuits as the
Vicar, and would certainly enjoy them better;
and anyhow it was a disputable point, and no
business of mine. Nature, who had accepted

me for ally, cared little who had the world's biscuits, and assuredly was not going to let any friend of hers waste his time in playing policeman for Society.

He was tugging at me anew, my insistent guide; and I felt sure, as I rambled off in his wake, that he had more holiday matter to show me. And so, indeed, he had; and all of it was to the same lawless tune. Like a black pirate flag on the blue ocean of air, a hawk hung ominous; then, plummet-wise, dropped to the hedgerow, whence there rose, thin and shrill, a piteous voice of squealing. By the time I got there a whisk of feathers on the turf—like scattered playbills—was all that remained to tell of the tragedy just enacted. Yet Nature smiled and sang on, pitiless, gay, impartial. To her, who took no sides, there was every bit as much to be said for the hawk as for the chaffinch. Both were her children, and she would show no preferences.

Further on, a hedgehog lay dead athwart the path—nay, more than dead; decadent, distinctly; a sorry sight for one that had known the fellow in more bustling circumstances. Nature might at least have paused to shed one

tear over this rough-jacketed little son of hers,
for his wasted aims, his cancelled ambitions,
his whole career of usefulness cut suddenly
short. But not a bit of it! Jubilant as ever,
her song went bubbling on, and 'Death-in-
Life'—and again, 'Life-in-Death,' were its
alternate burdens. And looking round, and
seeing the sheep-nibbled heels of turnips that
dotted the ground, their hearts eaten out of
them in frost-bound days now over and
done, I seemed to discern, faintly, a something of the stern meaning in her valorous
chant.

My invisible companion was singing also,
and seemed at times to be chuckling softly to
himself,—doubtless at thought of the strange
new lessons he was teaching me; perhaps, too,
at a special bit of waggishness he had still in
store. For when at last he grew weary of such
insignificant earth-bound company, he deserted
me at a certain spot I knew; then dropped,
subsided, and slunk away into nothingness.
I raised my eyes, and before me, grim and
lichened, stood the ancient whipping-post of
the village; its sides fretted with the initials
of a generation that scorned its mute lesson,

but still clipped by the stout rusty shackles
that had tethered the wrists of such of that
generation's ancestors as had dared to mock
at order and law. Had I been an infant
Sterne, here was a grand chance for senti-
mental output! As things were, I could only
hurry homewards, my moral tail well between
my legs, with an uneasy feeling, as I glanced
back over my shoulder, that there was more
in this chance than met the eye.

And outside our gate I found Charlotte,
alone and crying. Edward, it seemed, had
persuaded her to hide, in the full expectation
of being duly found and ecstatically pounced
upon ; then he had caught sight of the butcher's
cart, and, forgetting his obligations, had rushed
off for a ride. Harold, it further appeared, greatly
coveting tadpoles, and top-heavy with the eager-
ness of possession, had fallen into the pond.
This, in itself, was nothing ; but on attempting
to sneak in by the back-door, he had rendered
up his duckweed-bedabbled person into the
hands of an aunt, and had been promptly sent
off to bed ; and this, on a holiday, was very
much. The moral of the whipping-post was
working itself out ; and I was not in the least

surprised when, on reaching home, I was seized
upon and accused of doing something I had
never even thought of. And my frame of
mind was such, that I could only wish most
heartily that I had done it.

A WHITE-WASHED UNCLE

IN our small lives that day was eventful when another uncle was to come down from town, and submit his character and qualifications (albeit unconsciously) to our careful criticism. Earlier uncles had been weighed in the balance, and—alas!—found grievously wanting. There was Uncle Thomas—a failure from the first. Not that his disposition was malevolent, nor were his habits such as to unfit him for decent society; but his rooted conviction seemed to be that the reason of a child's existence was to serve as a butt for senseless adult jokes—or what, from the accompanying guffaws of laughter, appeared to be intended for jokes. Now, we were anxious that he should have a perfectly fair trial; so in the tool-house, between breakfast and lessons, we discussed and examined all his witticisms one by one, calmly, critically, dispassionately. It was no good: we could not discover any salt in them. And as only a genuine gift of humour could have saved Uncle Thomas—for he pretended to naught besides—he was reluctantly writ down a hopeless impostor.

Uncle George—the youngest—was distinctly more promising. He accompanied us cheerily round the establishment—suffered himself to be introduced to each of the cows—held out the right hand of fellowship to the pig—and even hinted that a pair of pink-eyed Himalayan rabbits might arrive—unexpectedly—from town some day. We were just considering whether in this fertile soil an apparently accidental remark on the solid qualities of guinea-pigs or ferrets might haply blossom and bring forth fruit, when our governess appeared on the scene. Uncle George's manner at once underwent a complete and contemptible change. His interest in rational topics seemed, 'like a fountain's sickening pulse,' to flag and ebb away; and though Miss Smedley's ostensible purpose was to take Selina for her usual walk, I can vouch for it that Selina spent her morning ratting, along with the keeper's boy and me; while if Miss Smedley walked with any one,

it would appear to have been with Uncle
George.

But, despicable as his conduct had been, he
underwent no hasty condemnation. The defec-
tion was discussed in all its bearings, but it
seemed sadly clear at last that this uncle must
possess some innate badness of character and
fondness for low company. We who from daily
experience knew Miss Smedley like a book—
were we not only too well aware that she had
neither accomplishments nor charms—no characteristic, in fact, but an inbred viciousness of
temper and disposition? True, she knew the
dates of the English kings by heart; but how
could that profit Uncle George, who, having
passed into the army, had ascended beyond the
need of useful information? Our bows and
arrows, on the other hand, had been freely
placed at his disposal; and a soldier should not
have hesitated in his choice a moment. No:
Uncle George had fallen from grace, and was
unanimously damned. And the non-arrival of
the Himalayan rabbits was only another nail
in his coffin. Uncles, therefore, were just then
a heavy and lifeless market, and there was
little inclination to deal. Still it was agreed

that Uncle William, who had just returned from India, should have as fair a trial as the others ; more especially as romantic possibilities might well be embodied in one who had held the gorgeous East in fee.

Selina had kicked my shins—like the girl she is !—during a scuffle in the passage, and I was still rubbing them with one hand when I found that the uncle-on-approbation was half-heartedly shaking the other. A florid, elderly man, quite unmistakably nervous, he let drop one grimy paw after another, and, turning very red, with an awkward simulation of heartiness, ' Well, h' are y' all ? ' he said, ' Glad to see me, eh ? ' As we could hardly, in justice, be expected to have formed an opinion on him at that early stage, we could but look at each other in silence; which scarce served to relieve the tension of the situation. Indeed, the cloud never really lifted during his stay. In talking things over later, some one put forward the suggestion that he must at some time or other have committed a stupendous crime. But I could not bring myself to believe that the man, though evidently un-happy, was really guilty of anything; and I caught him once or twice looking at us with evident kindliness, though, seeing himself observed, he blushed and turned away his head.

When at last the atmosphere was clear of his depressing influence, we met despondently in the potato-cellar—all of us, that is, but Harold, who had been told off to accompany his relative to the station ; and the feeling was unanimous that, as an uncle, William could not be allowed to pass. Selina roundly declared him a beast, pointing out that he had not even got us a half-holiday ; and, indeed, there seemed little to do but to pass sentence. We were about to put it to the vote, when Harold appeared on the scene ; his red face, round eyes, and mysterious demeanour, hinting at awful portents. Speechless he stood a space : then, slowly drawing his hand from the pocket of his knickerbockers, he displayed on a dirty palm one—two—three—four half-crowns ! We could but gaze—tranced, breathless, mute. Never had any of us seen, in the aggregate, so much bullion before. Then Harold told his tale.

'I took the old fellow to the station,' he said, 'and as we went along I told him all about the stationmaster's family, and how I had seen the porter kissing our housemaid, and what a nice

fellow he was, with no airs or affectation about
him, and anything I thought would be of
interest; but he didn't seem to pay much
attention, but walked along puffing his cigar,
and once I thought—I'm not certain, but I
thought—I heard him say, "Well, thank God,
that's over!" When we got to the station he
stopped suddenly, and said, "Hold on a minute!"
Then he shoved these into my hand in a
frightened sort of way, and said, "Look here,
youngster! These are for you and the other
kids. Buy what you like—make little beasts
of yourselves—only don't tell the old people,
mind! Now cut away home!" So I cut.'

A solemn hush fell on the assembly, broken
first by the small Charlotte. 'I didn't know,'
she observed dreamily, 'that there were such
good men anywhere in the world. I hope he'll
die to-night, for then he'll go straight to heaven!'
But the repentant Selina bewailed herself with
tears and sobs, refusing to be comforted; for
that in her haste she had called this white-souled
relative a beast.

'I'll tell you what we'll do,' said Edward, the
master-mind, rising—as he always did—to the
situation : 'We'll christen the piebald pig after

him—the one that hasn't got a name yet. And that 'll show we 're sorry for our mistake!'

'I—I christened that pig this morning,' Harold guiltily confessed ; 'I christened it after the curate. I 'm very sorry—but he came and bowled to me last night, after you others had all been sent to bed early—and somehow I felt I *had* to do it!'

'Oh, but that doesn't count,' said Edward hastily ; 'because we weren't all there. We 'll take that christening off, and call it Uncle William. And you can save up the curate for the next litter!'

And the motion being agreed to without a division, the House went into Committee of Supply.

ALARUMS AND EXCURSIONS

'LET's pretend,' suggested Harold, 'that we're Cavaliers and Roundheads; and *you* be a Roundhead!'

'O bother,' I replied drowsily, 'we pretended that yesterday; and it's not my turn to be a Roundhead, anyhow.' The fact is, I was lazy, and the call to arms fell on indifferent ears. We three younger ones were stretched at length in the orchard. The sun was hot, the season merry June, and never (I thought) had there been such wealth and riot of buttercups throughout the lush grass. Green-and-gold was the dominant key that day. Instead of active 'pretence' with its shouts and its perspiration, how much better—I held—to lie at ease and pretend to one's self, in green and golden fancies, slipping the husk and passing, a careless lounger, through a sleepy imaginary world all gold and green! But the persistent Harold was not to be fobbed off.

'Well then,' he began afresh, 'let's pretend we're Knights of the Round Table; and (with a rush) *I'll* be Lancelot!'

'I won't play unless I'm Lancelot,' I said. I didn't mean it really, but the game of Knights always began with this particular contest.

'O *please*,' implored Harold. 'You know when Edward's here I never get a chance of being Lancelot. I haven't been Lancelot for weeks!'

Then I yielded gracefully. 'All right,' I said. 'I'll be Tristram.'

'O, but you can't,' cried Harold again. 'Charlotte has always been Tristram. She won't play unless she's allowed to be Tristram! Be somebody else this time.'

Charlotte said nothing, but breathed hard, looking straight before her. The peerless hunter and harper was her special hero of romance, and rather than see the part in less appreciative hands, she would have gone back in tears to the stuffy schoolroom.

'I don't care,' I said: 'I'll be anything. I'll be Sir Kay. Come on!'

Then once more in this country's story the mail-clad knights paced through the greenwood

shaw, questing adventure, redressing wrong;
and bandits, five to one, broke and fled discomfited to their caves. Once more were
damsels rescued, dragons disembowelled, and
giants, in every corner of the orchard, deprived
of their already superfluous number of heads;
while Palomides the Saracen waited for us by
the well, and Sir Breuse Saunce Pité vanished
in craven flight before the skilled spear that
was his terror and his bane. Once more the
lists were dight in Camelot, and all was gay
with shimmer of silk and gold; the earth shook
with thunder of hooves, ash-staves flew in
splinters, and the firmament rang to the clash
of sword on helm. The varying fortune of the
day swung doubtful—now on this side, now
on that; till at last Lancelot, grim and great,
thrusting through the press, unhorsed Sir
Tristram (an easy task), and bestrode her,
threatening doom; while the Cornish knight,
forgetting hard-won fame of old, cried piteously,
'You're hurting me, I tell you! and you're
tearing my frock!' Then it happed that Sir
Kay, hurtling to the rescue, stopped short in
his stride, catching sight suddenly, through
apple-boughs, of a gleam of scarlet afar off;

while the confused tramp of many horses,
mingled with talk and laughter, was borne to
the ears of his fellow-champions and himself.

'What is it?' inquired Tristram, sitting up
and shaking out her curls; while Lancelot
forsook the clanging lists and trotted nimbly
to the boundary-hedge.

I stood spell-bound for a moment longer, and
then, with a cry of 'Soldiers!' I was off to the
hedge, Sir Tristram picking herself up and
scurrying after us.

Down the road they came, two and two,
at an easy walk; scarlet flamed in the eye,
bits jingled and saddles squeaked delightfully;
while the men, in a halo of dust, smoked their
short clays like the heroes they were. In a
swirl of intoxicating glory the troop clinked
and clattered by, while we shouted and waved,
jumping up and down, and the big jolly horse-
men acknowledged the salute with easy con-
descension. The moment they were past
we were through the hedge and after them.
Soldiers were not the common stuff of everyday
life. There had been nothing like this since the
winter before last, when on a certain afternoon
—bare of leaf and monochromatic in its hue

of sodden fallow and frost-nipt copse—suddenly
the hounds had burst through the fence with
their mellow cry, and all the paddock was for
the minute reverberant of thudding hoof and
dotted with glancing red.   But this was better,
since it could only mean that blows and blood-
shed were in the air.

'Is there going to be a battle?' panted
Harold, hardly able to keep up for excitement.

'Of course there is,' I replied.   'We're just
in time.   Come on!'

Perhaps I ought to have known better; and
yet——? The pigs and poultry, with whom we
chiefly consorted, could instruct us little concerning the peace that lapped in these latter
days our seagirt realm.   In the schoolroom
we were just now dallying with the Wars of the
Roses; and did not legends of the country-side
inform us how cavaliers had once galloped up
and down these very lanes from their quarters
in the village?   Here, now, were soldiers
unmistakable; and if their business was not
fighting, what was it?   Sniffing the joy of
battle, we followed hard in their tracks.

'Won't Edward be sorry,' puffed Harold,
'that he's begun that beastly Latin?'

It did, indeed, seem hard. Edward, the most martial spirit of us all, was drearily conjugating *amo* (of all verbs!) between four walls; while Selina, who ever thrilled ecstatic to a red coat, was struggling with the uncouth German tongue. 'Age,' I reflected, 'carries its penalties.'

It was a grievous disappointment to us that the troop passed through the village unmolested. Every cottage, I pointed out to my companions, ought to have been loopholed, and strongly held. But no opposition was offered to the soldiers: who, indeed, conducted themselves with a recklessness and a want of precaution that seemed simply criminal.

At the last cottage a transitory gleam of common sense flickered across me, and, turning on Charlotte, I sternly ordered her back. The small maiden, docile but exceedingly dolorous, dragged reluctant feet homewards, heavy at heart that she was to behold no stout fellows slain that day; but Harold and I held steadily on, expecting every instant to see the environing hedges crackle and spit forth the leaden death.

'Will they be Indians?' asked my brother

(meaning the enemy) 'or Roundheads, or what?'

I reflected. Harold always required direct straightforward answers—not faltering suppositions.

'They won't be Indians,' I replied at last; 'nor yet Roundheads. There haven't been any Roundheads seen about here for a long time. They'll be Frenchmen.'

Harold's face fell. 'All right,' he said: 'Frenchmen'll do; but I did hope they'd be Indians.'

'If they were going to be Indians,' I explained, 'I — I don't think I'd go on. Because when Indians take you prisoner they scalp you first, and then burn you at the stake. But Frenchmen don't do that sort of thing.'

'Are you quite sure?' asked Harold doubtfully.

'Quite,' I replied. 'Frenchmen only shut you up in a thing called the Bastille; and then you get a file sent in to you in a loaf of bread, and saw the bars through, and slide down a rope, and they all fire at you—but they don't hit you—and you run down to the seashore as hard as you can, and swim off to a British frigate, and there you are!'

Harold brightened up again. The programme was rather attractive. 'If they try to take us prisoner,' he said, 'we—we won't run, will we?'

Meanwhile, the craven foe was a long time showing himself; and we were reaching strange outland country, uncivilised, wherein lions might be expected to prowl at nightfall. I had a stitch in my side, and both Harold's stockings had come down. Just as I was beginning to have gloomy doubts of the proverbial courage of Frenchmen, the officer called out something, the men closed up, and, breaking into a trot, the troops—already far ahead—vanished out of our sight. With a sinking at the heart, I began to suspect we had been fooled.

'Are they charging?' cried Harold, very weary, but rallying gamely.

'I think not,' I replied doubtfully. 'When there's going to be a charge, the officer always makes a speech, and then they draw their swords and the trumpets blow, and——but let's try a short cut. We may catch them up yet.'

So we struck across the fields and into

another road, and pounded down that, and then over more fields, panting, down-hearted, yet hoping for the best. The sun went in, and a thin drizzle began to fall; we were muddy, breathless, almost dead-beat; but we blundered on, till at last we struck a road more brutally, more callously unfamiliar than any road I ever looked upon. Not a hint nor a sign of friendly direction or assistance on the dogged white face of it! There was no longer any disguising it: we were hopelessly lost. The small rain continued steadily, the evening began to come on. Really there are moments when a fellow is justified in crying; and I would have cried too, if Harold had not been there. That right-minded child regarded an elder brother as a veritable god; and I could see that he felt himself as secure as if a whole Brigade of Guards had hedged him round with protecting bayonets. But I dreaded sore lest he should begin again with his questions.

As I gazed in dumb appeal on the face of unresponsive nature, the sound of nearing wheels sent a pulse of hope through my being: increasing to rapture as I recognised in the approaching vehicle the familiar carriage of

the old doctor. If ever a god emerged from
a machine, it was when this heaven-sent friend,
recognising us, stopped and jumped out with a
cheery hail. Harold rushed up to him at once.
'Have you been there?' he cried. 'Was it a
jolly fight? who beat? were there many people
killed?'

The doctor appeared puzzled. I briefly
explained the situation.

'I see,' said the doctor, looking grave and
twisting his face this way and that. 'Well,
the fact is, there isn't going to be any battle
to-day. It's been put off, on account of the
change in the weather. You will have due
notice of the renewal of hostilities. And now
you'd better jump in and I'll drive you home.
You've been running a fine rig! Why, you
might have both been taken and shot as spies!'

This special danger had never even occurred
to us. The thrill of it accentuated the cosy
homelike feeling of the cushions we nestled into
as we rolled homewards. The doctor beguiled
the journey with blood-curdling narratives of
personal adventure in the tented field, he having
followed the profession of arms (so it seemed)
in every quarter of the globe. Time, the

destroyer of all things beautiful, subsequently revealed the baselessness of these legends; but what of that? There are higher things than truth; and we were almost reconciled, by the time we were put down at our gate, to the fact that the battle had been postponed.

THE FINDING OF THE
PRINCESS

IT was the day I was promoted to a tooth-brush. The girls, irrespective of age, had been thus distinguished some time before; why, we boys could never rightly understand, except that it was part and parcel of a system of studied favouritism on behalf of creatures both physically inferior and (as was shown by a fondness for tale-bearing) of weaker mental fibre to us boys. It was not that we yearned after these strange instruments in themselves. Edward, indeed, applied his to the scrubbing-out of his squirrel's cage, and for personal use, when a superior eye was grim on him, borrowed Harold's or mine, indifferently. But the nimbus of distinction that clung to them—that we coveted exceedingly. What more, indeed, was there to ascend to, before the remote, but still possible, razor and strop?

Perhaps the exaltation had mounted to my head; or nature and the perfect morning joined to hint at disaffection. Anyhow, having breakfasted, and triumphantly repeated the collect I had broken down in the last Sunday—'twas one without rhythm or alliteration: a most objectionable collect — having achieved thus much, the small natural man in me rebelled, and I vowed, as I straddled and spat about the stable-yard in feeble imitation of the coachman, that lessons might go to the Inventor of them. It was only geography that morning, any way: and the practical thing was worth any quantity of bookish theoric. As for me, I was going on my travels, and imports and exports, populations and capitals, might very well wait while I explored the breathing coloured world outside.

True, a fellow-rebel was wanted; and Harold might, as a rule, have been counted on with certainty. But just then Harold was very proud. The week before he had 'gone into tables,' and had been endowed with a new slate, having a miniature sponge attached wherewith we washed the faces of Charlotte's dolls, thereby producing an unhealthy pallor which struck terror into the child's heart, always timorous regarding epidemic visitations. As to 'tables,' nobody knew exactly what they were, least of all Harold; but it was a step over the heads of the rest, and therefore a subject for self-adulation and—generally speaking—airs; so that Harold, hugging his slate and his chains, was out of the question now. In such a matter, girls were worse than useless, as wanting the necessary tenacity of will and contempt for self-constituted authority. So eventually I slipped through the hedge a solitary protestant, and issued forth on the lane what time the rest of the civilised world was sitting down to lessons.

The scene was familiar enough; and yet, this morning, how different it all seemed! The act, with its daring, tinted everything with new strange hues; affecting the individual with a sort of bruised feeling just below the pit of the stomach, that was intensified whenever his thoughts flew back to the ink-stained smelly schoolroom. And could this be really me? or was I only contemplating, from the schoolroom aforesaid, some other jolly young mutineer, faring forth under the genial sun? Anyhow, here was the friendly well, in its old place, half-way up the lane. Hither the yoke-shouldering village-folk were wont to come to fill their clinking buckets; when the drippings made worms of wet in the thick dust of the road. They had flat wooden crosses inside each pail, which floated on the top and (we were instructed) served to prevent the water from slopping over. We used to wonder by what magic this strange principle worked, and who first invented the crosses, and whether he got a peerage for it. But indeed the well was a centre of mystery, for a hornet's nest was somewhere hard by, and the very thought was fearsome. Wasps we knew well and disdained, storming them in their fastnesses. But these great Beasts, vestured in angry orange, three stings from which—so 'twas averred—would kill a horse, these were of a different kidney, and their dreadful drone suggested prudence and retreat. At this time neither villagers nor hornets encroached on the stillness: lessons, apparently, pervaded all nature. So, after dabbling awhile in the well—what boy has ever passed a bit of water without messing in it?— I scrambled through the hedge, shunning the hornet-haunted side, and struck into the silence of the copse.

If the lane had been deserted, this was loneliness become personal. Here mystery lurked and peeped; here brambles caught and held you with a purpose of their own; here saplings whipped your face with human spite. The copse, too, proved vaster in extent, more direfully drawn out, than one would ever have guessed from its frontage on the lane: and I was really glad when at last the wood opened and sloped down to a streamlet brawling forth into the sunlight. By this cheery companion I wandered along, conscious of little but that Nature, in providing store of water-rats, had thoughtfully furnished provender of right-sized stones. Rapids, also, there were, telling of canoes and portages—crinkling bays and inlets —caves for pirates and hidden treasures—the wise Dame had forgotten nothing—till at last, after what lapse of time I know not, my further course, though not the stream's, was barred by some six feet of stout wire netting, stretched from side to side just where a thick hedge, arching till it touched, forbade all further view.

The excitement of the thing was becoming thrilling. A Black Flag must surely be fluttering close by? Here was most plainly a malignant contrivance of the Pirates, designed to baffle our gun-boats when we dashed up-stream to shell them from their lair! A gun-boat, indeed, might well have hesitated, so stout was the netting, so close the hedge. But I spied where a rabbit was wont to pass, close down by the water's edge; where a rabbit could go a boy could follow, howbeit stomach-wise and with one leg in the stream; so the passage was achieved, and I stood inside, safe but breathless at the sight.

Gone was the brambled waste, gone the flickering tangle of woodland. Instead, terrace after terrace of shaven sward, stone-edged, urn-cornered, stepped delicately down to where the stream, now tamed and educated, passed from one to another marble basin, in which on occasion gleams of red hinted at gold-fish poised among the spreading water-lilies. The scene lay silent and slumbrous in the brooding noonday sun: the drowsing peacock squatted humped on the lawn, no fish leaped in the pools, no bird declared himself from the trim secluding hedges. Self-confessed it was here, then, at last, the Garden of Sleep!

Two things, in those old days, I held in especial distrust: gamekeepers and gardeners. Seeing, however, no baleful apparitions of either quality, I pursued my way between rich flower-beds, in search of the necessary Princess. Conditions declared her presence patently as trumpets; without this centre such surroundings could not exist. A pavilion, gold-topped, wreathed with lush jessamine, beckoned with a special significance over close-set shrubs. There, if anywhere, She should be enshrined. Instinct, and some knowledge of the habits of princesses, triumphed; for (indeed) there She was! In no tranced repose, however, but laughingly, struggling to disengage her hand from the grasp of a grown-up man who occupied the marble bench with her. (As to age, I suppose now that the two swung in respective scales that pivoted on twenty. But children heed no minor distinctions. To them, the inhabited world is composed of the two main divisions: children and upgrown people; the latter in no way superior to the former—only hopelessly different. These two, then, belonged to the grown-up section.) I paused, thinking it strange they should prefer seclusion when there were fish to be caught, and butterflies to hunt in the sun outside; and as I cogitated thus, the grown-up man caught sight of me.

'Hallo, sprat!' he said with some abruptness; 'Where do you spring from?'

'I came up the stream,' I explained politely and comprehensively, 'and I was only looking for the Princess.'

'Then you are a water-baby,' he replied. 'And what do you think of the Princess, now you've found her?'

'I think she is lovely,' I said (and doubtless I was right, having never learned to flatter). 'But she's wide-awake, so I suppose somebody has kissed her!'

This very natural deduction moved the grown-up man to laughter; but the Princess, turning red and jumping up, declared that it was time for lunch.

'Come along, then,' said the grown-up man; 'and you too, water-baby. Come and have something solid. You must want it.'

I accompanied them without any feeling of false delicacy. The world, as known to me, was spread with food each several mid-day, and the particular table one sat at seemed a

matter of no importance.   The palace was
very sumptuous and beautiful, just what a
palace ought to be; and we were met by a
stately lady, rather more grown-up than the
Princess—apparently her mother.   My friend
the Man was very kind, and introduced me
as the Captain, saying I had just run down
from Aldershot.   I didn't know where Aldershot was, but I had no manner of doubt that
he was perfectly right.   As a rule, indeed,
grown-up people are fairly correct on matters
of fact; it is in the higher gift of imagination
that they are so sadly to seek.

The lunch was excellent and varied.   Another gentleman in beautiful clothes—a lord
presumably—lifted me into a high carved
chair, and stood behind it, brooding over me
like a Providence.   I endeavoured to explain
who I was and where I had come from, and
to impress the company with my own tooth-
brush and Harold's tables; but either they
were stupid—or is it a characteristic of Fairyland that every one laughs at the most ordinary
remarks?   My friend the Man said good-
naturedly, 'All right, Water-baby; you came
up the stream, and that's good enough for us.'

The lord—a reserved sort of man, I thought—took no share in the conversation.

After lunch I walked on the terrace with the Princess and my friend the Man, and was very proud. And I told him what I was going to be, and he told me what he was going to be; and then I remarked, 'I suppose you two are going to get married?' He only laughed, after the Fairy fashion. 'Because if you aren't,' I added, 'you really ought to': meaning only that a man who discovered a Princess, living in the right sort of Palace like this, and didn't marry her there and then, was false to all recognised tradition.

They laughed again, and my friend suggested I should go down to the pond and look at the gold-fish, while they went for a stroll. I was sleepy, and assented; but before they left me, the grown-up man put two half-crowns in my hand, for the purpose, he explained, of treating the other water-babies. I was so touched by this crowning mark of friendship that I nearly cried; and I thought much more of his generosity than of the fact that the Princess, ere she moved away, stooped down and kissed me.

I watched them disappear down the path—
how naturally arms seem to go round waists
in Fairyland!—and then, my cheek on the
cool marble, lulled by the trickle of water, I
slipped into dreamland out of real and magic
world alike. When I woke, the sun had gone
in, a chill wind set all the leaves a-whispering,
and the peacock on the lawn was harshly
calling up the rain. A wild unreasoning panic
possessed me, and I sped out of the garden like
a guilty thing, wriggled through the rabbit-
run, and threaded my doubtful way homewards, hounded by nameless terrors. The
half-crowns happily remained solid and real
to the touch; but could I hope to bear such
treasure safely through the brigand-haunted
wood? It was a dirty, weary little object
that entered its home, at nightfall, by the
unassuming aid of the scullery-window: and
only to be sent tealess to bed seemed infinite
mercy to him. Officially tealess, that is; for,
as was usual after such escapades, a sympathetic housemaid, coming delicately by back-
stairs, stayed him with chunks of cold pudding
and condolence, till his small skin was tight
as any drum. Then, nature asserting herself,

I passed into the comforting kingdom of sleep, where, a golden carp of fattest build, I oared it in translucent waters with a new half-crown snug under right fin and left; and thrust up a nose through water-lily leaves to be kissed by a rose-flushed Princess.

SAWDUST AND SIN

A BELT of rhododendrons grew close down to one side of our pond ; and along the edge of it many things flourished rankly. If you crept through the undergrowth and crouched by the water's rim, it was easy—if your imagination were in healthy working order—to transport yourself in a trice to the heart of a tropical forest. Overhead the monkeys chattered, parrots flashed from bough to bough, strange large blossoms shone all round you, and the push and rustle of great beasts moving unseen thrilled you deliciously. And if you lay down with your nose an inch or two from the water, it was not long ere the old sense of proportion vanished clean away. The glittering insects that darted to and fro on its surface became sea-monsters dire, the gnats that hung above them swelled to albatrosses, and the pond itself stretched out into a vast inland sea, whereon a

navy might ride secure, and whence at any
moment the hairy scalp of a sea-serpent might
be seen to emerge.

It is impossible, however, to play at tropical
forests properly, when homely accents of the
human voice intrude; and all my hopes of
seeing a tiger seized by a crocodile while
drinking (*vide* picture-books, *passim*) vanished
abruptly, and earth resumed her old dimensions,
when the sound of Charlotte's prattle somewhere
hard by broke in on my primæval seclusion.
Looking out from the bushes, I saw her trotting
towards an open space of lawn the other side
the pond, chattering to herself in her accustomed
fashion, a doll tucked under either arm, and her
brow knit with care. Propping up her double
burthen against a friendly stump, she sat down
in front of them, as full of worry and anxiety
as a Chancellor on a Budget night.

Her victims, who stared resignedly in front
of them, were recognisable as Jerry and Rosa.
Jerry hailed from far Japan: his hair was
straight and black, his one garment cotton of
a simple blue; and his reputation was distinctly
bad. Jerome was his proper name, from his
supposed likeness to the holy man who hung in

a print on the staircase; though a shaven crown was the only thing in common 'twixt Western saint and Eastern sinner. Rosa was typical British, from her flaxen poll to the stout calves she displayed so liberally; and in character she was of the blameless order of those who have not yet been found out.

I suspected Jerry from the first. There was a latent devilry in his slant eyes as he sat there moodily; and knowing what he was capable of, I scented trouble in store for Charlotte. Rosa I was not so sure about; she sat demurely and upright, and looked far away into the tree-tops in a visionary, world-forgetting sort of way; yet the prim purse of her mouth was somewhat overdone, and her eyes glittered unnaturally.

'Now, I'm going to begin where I left off,' said Charlotte, regardless of stops, and thumping the turf with her fist excitedly: 'and you must pay attention, 'cos this is a treat, to have a story told you before you're put to bed. Well, so the White Rabbit scuttled off down the passage and Alice hoped he'd come back 'cos he had a waistcoat on and her flamingo flew up a tree—but we haven't got to that part yet you must wait a minute, and—where had I got to?'

Jerry only remained passive until Charlotte had got well under way, and then began to heel over quietly in Rosa's direction. His head fell on her plump shoulder, causing her to start nervously.

Charlotte seized and shook him with vigour. 'O Jerry,' she cried piteously, 'if you're not going to be good, how ever shall I tell you my story?'

Jerry's face was injured innocence itself. 'Blame if you like, Madam,' he seemed to say, 'the eternal laws of gravitation, but not a helpless puppet, who is also an orphan and a stranger in the land.'

'Now we'll go on,' began Charlotte once more. 'So she got into the garden at last— I've left out a lot but you won't care, I'll tell you some other time—and they were all playing croquet, and that's where the flamingo comes in, and the Queen shouted out, "Off with her head!"'

At this point Jerry collapsed forward, suddenly and completely, his bald pate between his knees. Charlotte was not very angry this time. The sudden development of tragedy in the story had evidently been too much for the poor fellow. She straightened him out, wiped his nose, and, after trying him in various positions, to which he refused to adapt himself, she propped him against the shoulder of the (apparently) unconscious Rosa. Then my eyes were opened, and the full measure of Jerry's infamy became apparent. This, then, was what he had been playing up for! The rascal had designs, had he? I resolved to keep him under close observation.

'If you'd been in the garden,' went on Charlotte reproachfully, 'and flopped down like that when the Queen said "Off with his head!" she'd have offed with your head; but Alice wasn't that sort of girl at all. She just said, "I'm not afraid of you, you're nothing but a pack of cards"—O dear! I've got to the end already, and I hadn't begun hardly! I never can make my stories last out! Never mind, I'll tell you another one.'

Jerry didn't seem to care, now he had gained his end, whether the stories lasted out or not. He was nestling against Rosa's plump form with a look of satisfaction that was simply idiotic; and one arm had disappeared from view—was it round her waist? Rosa's natural blush seemed deeper than usual, her head inclined shyly—it must have been round her waist.

'If it wasn't so near your bedtime,' continued Charlotte reflectively, 'I'd tell you a nice story with a bogy in it. But you'd be frightened, and you'd dream of bogies all night. So I'll tell you one about a White Bear, only you mustn't scream when the bear says 'Wow,' like I used to, 'cos he's a good bear really——'

Here Rosa fell flat on her back in the deadest of faints. Her limbs were rigid, her eyes glassy. What had Jerry been doing? It must have been something very bad, for her to take on like that. I scrutinised him carefully, while Charlotte ran to comfort the damsel. He appeared to be whistling a tune and regarding the scenery. If I only possessed Jerry's command of feature, I thought to myself, half regretfully, I would never be found out in anything.

'It's all your fault, Jerry,' said Charlotte reproachfully, when the lady had been restored to consciousness: 'Rosa's as good as gold except when you make her wicked. I'd put you in the corner, only a stump hasn't got a corner—wonder why that is? Thought every-

thing had corners.   Never mind, you'll have to
sit with your face to the wall—*so*. Now you
can sulk if you like!'

Jerry seemed to hesitate a moment between
the bliss of indulgence in sulks with a sense of
injury, and the imperious summons of beauty
waiting to be wooed at his elbow; then, over-
mastered by his passion, he fell sideways across
Rosa's lap. One arm stuck stiffly upwards, as
in passionate protestation; his amorous countenance was full of entreaty.   Rosa hesitated—
wavered — yielded, crushing his slight frame
under the weight of her full-bodied surrender.

Charlotte had stood a good deal, but it was
possible to abuse even her patience. Snatching
Jerry from his lawless embraces, she reversed
him across her knee, and then—the outrage
offered to the whole superior sex in Jerry's
hapless person was too painful to witness; but
though I turned my head away the sound of
brisk slaps continued to reach my tingling ears.
When I dared to look again, Jerry was sitting
up as before; his garment, somewhat crumpled,
was restored to its original position; but his
pallid countenance was set hard. Knowing as I
did, only too well, what a volcano of passion and

shame must be seething under that impassive exterior, for the moment I felt sorry for him.

Rosa's face was still buried in her frock; it might have been shame, it might have been grief for Jerry's sufferings. But the callous Japanese never even looked her way. His heart was exceeding bitter within him. In merely following up his natural impulses he had run his head against convention, and learned how hard a thing it was; and the sunshiny world was all black to him. Even Charlotte softened somewhat at the sight of his rigid misery. 'If you'll say you're sorry, Jerome,' she said, 'I'll say I'm sorry, too.'

Jerry only dropped his shoulders against the stump and stared out in the direction of his dear native Japan, where love was no sin, and smacking had not been introduced. Why had he ever left it? He would go back to-morrow! And yet there were obstacles: another grievance. Nature, in endowing Jerry with every grace of form and feature, along with a sensitive soul, had somehow forgotten the gift of loco-motion.

There was a crackling in the bushes behind me, with sharp short pants as of a small steam-

engine, and Rollo, the black retriever, just
released from his chain by some friendly hand,
burst through the underwood, seeking congenial
company.   I joyfully hailed him to stop and be
a panther, but he sped away round the pond,
upset Charlotte with a boisterous caress, and
seizing Jerry by the middle, disappeared with
him down the drive.   Charlotte panting, raved
behind the swift-footed avenger of crime ; Rosa
lay dishevelled, bereft of consciousness ; Jerry
himself spread helpless arms to heaven, and I
almost thought I heard a cry for mercy, a tardy
promise of amendment.   But it was too late.
The Black Man had got Jerry at last; and
though the tear of sensibility might bedew an
eye or two for his lost sake, no one who really
knew him could deny the justice of his fate.

'YOUNG ADAM CUPID'

NOBODY would have suspected Edward of being in love, had it not been that after breakfast, with an overacted carelessness, 'Anybody who likes,' he said, 'can feed my rabbits,' and he disappeared, with a jauntiness that deceived nobody, in the direction of the orchard. Now kingdoms might totter and reel, and convulsions play skittles with the map of Europe; but the iron unwritten law prevailed, that each boy severely fed his own rabbits. There was good ground, then, for suspicion and alarm; and while the lettuce leaves were being drawn through the wires, Harold and I conferred seriously on the situation.

It may be thought that the affair was none of our business; and indeed we cared little as individuals. We were only concerned as members of a corporation, for each of whom the mental or physical ailment of one of his fellows might have far-reaching effects. It was thought best that Harold, as least open to suspicion of motive, should be despatched to probe and peer. His instructions were, to proceed by a report on the health of our rabbits in particular; to glide gently into a discussion concerning rabbits in general, their customs, practices, and vices; and to pass thence, by a natural transition, to the female sex, the inherent flaws in its composition, and the reasons for regarding it (speaking broadly) as dirt. He was especially to be very diplomatic, and then to return and report progress. He departed on his mission gaily; but his absence was short, and his return, discomfited and in tears, seemed to betoken some want of parts for diplomacy. He had found Edward, it appeared, pacing the orchard, with the sort of set smile that mountebanks wear in their precarious antics, fixed painfully on his face, as with pins. Harold had opened well, on the rabbit subject, but, with a fatal confusion between the abstract and the concrete, had then gone on to remark that Edward's lop-eared doe, with her long hindlegs and contemptuous twitch of the nose, always reminded him of Sabina Larkin (a nine-year-old damsel,

child of a neighbouring farmer): at which point
Edward, it would seem, had turned upon and
savagely maltreated him, twisting his arm and
punching him in the short ribs. So that
Harold returned to the rabbit-hutches preceded
by long-drawn wails: anon wishing, with tears
and sobs, that he were a man, to kick his love-
lorn brother; anon lamenting that ever he had
been born.

I was not big enough to stand up to Edward
personally, so I had to console the sufferer by
allowing him to grease the wheels of the donkey-
cart—a luscious treat that had been specially
reserved for me, a week past, by the gardener's
boy, for putting in a good word on his behalf
with the new kitchen-maid. Harold was soon
all smiles and grease; and I was not, on the
whole, dissatisfied with the significant hint that
had been gained as to the *fons et origo mali.*

Fortunately, means were at hand for resolving
any doubts on the subject, since the morning
was Sunday, and already the bells were ringing
for church. Lest the connexion may not be
evident at first sight, I should explain that
the gloomy period of church - time, with its
enforced inaction and its lack of real interest—

passed, too, within sight of all that the village
held of fairest—was just the one when a young
man's fancies lightly turned to thoughts of love.
The rest of the week afforded no leisure for
such trifling; but in church—well, there was
really nothing else to do! True, noughts-and-
crosses might be indulged in on flyleaves of
prayer-books while the Litany dragged its slow
length along; but what balm or what solace
could be found for the Sermon? Naturally the
eye, wandering here and there among the serried
ranks, made bold untrammelled choice among
our fair fellow-supplicants. It was in this way
that, some months earlier, under the exceptional
strain of the Athanasian Creed, my roving
fancy had settled upon the baker's wife as a
fit object for a life-long devotion. Her riper
charms had conquered a heart which none of
her be-muslined tittering juniors had been
able to subdue; and that she was already
wedded had never occurred to me as any bar
to my affection. Edward's general demeanour,
then, during morning service was safe to convict
him; but there was also a special test for
the particular case. It happened that we sat
in a transept, and, the Larkins being behind

us, Edward's only chance of feasting on Sabina's charms was in the all-too fleeting interval when we swung round eastwards. I was not mistaken. During the singing of the Benedictus the impatient one made several false starts, and at last he slewed fairly round before 'As it was in the beginning, is now, and ever shall be' was half finished. The evidence was conclusive : a court of law could have desired no better.

The fact being patent, the next thing was to grapple with it ; and my mind was fully occupied during the sermon. There was really nothing unfair or unbrotherly in my attitude. A philosophic affection such as mine own, which clashed with nothing, was (I held) permissible ; but the volcanic passions in which Edward indulged about once a quarter were a serious interference with business. To make matters worse, next week there was a circus coming to the neighbourhood, to which we had all been strictly forbidden to go ; and without Edward no visit in contempt of law and orders could be successfully brought off. I had sounded him as to the circus on our way to church, and he had replied briefly that the very thought of a clown made him sick.

Morbidity could no further go.   But the sermon came to an end without any line of conduct having suggested itself; and I walked home in some depression, feeling sadly that Venus was in the ascendant and in direful opposition, while Auriga — the circus star—drooped declinant, perilously near the horizon.

By the irony of fate, Aunt Eliza, of all people, turned out to be the *Dea ex machinâ*. The thing fell out in this wise.   It was that lady's obnoxious practice to issue forth, of a Sunday afternoon, on a visit of state to such farmers and cottagers as dwelt at hand; on which occasion she was wont to hale a reluctant boy along with her, from the mixed motives of propriety and his soul's health.   Much cudgelling of brains, I suppose, had on that particular day made me torpid and unwary.   Anyhow, when a victim came to be sought for, I fell an easy prey, while the others fled scatheless and whooping.   Our first visit was to the Larkins. Here ceremonial might be viewed in its finest flower, and we conducted ourselves, like Queen Elizabeth when she trod the measure, 'high and disposedly.'   In the low oak-panelled parlour cake and currant wine were set forth, and, after courtesies and compliments exchanged, Aunt Eliza, greatly condescending, talked the fashions with Mrs. Larkin; while the farmer and I, perspiring with the unusual effort, exchanged remarks on the mutability of the weather and the steady fall in the price of corn. (Who would have thought, to hear us, that only two short days ago we had confronted each other on either side of a hedge? I triumphant, provocative, derisive? He flushed, wroth, cracking his whip, and volleying forth profanity? So powerful is all-subduing ceremony!) Sabina the while, demurely seated with a *Pilgrim's Progress* on her knee, and apparently absorbed in a brightly-coloured presentment of 'Apollyon Straddling Right across the Way,' eyed me at times with shy interest; but repelled all Aunt Eliza's advances with a frigid politeness for which I could not sufficiently admire her.

'It's surprising to me,' I heard my aunt remark presently, 'how my eldest nephew, Edward, despises little girls. I heard him tell Charlotte the other day that he wished he could exchange her for a pair of Japanese guinea-pigs. It made the poor child cry. Boys are so heartless!' (I saw Sabina stiffen as she sat, and her tip-tilted nose twitched scornfully.) 'Now this boy here——' (my soul descended into my very boots. Could the woman have intercepted any of my amorous glances at the baker's wife?) 'Now this boy,' my aunt went on, 'is more human altogether. Only yesterday he took his sister to the baker's shop, and spent his only penny buying her sweets. I thought it showed such a nice disposition. I wish Edward were more like him!'

I breathed again. It was unnecessary to explain my real motives for that visit to the baker's. Sabina's face softened, and her contemptuous nose descended from its altitude of scorn; she gave me one shy glance of kindness, and then concentrated her attention upon Mercy knocking at the Wicket Gate. I felt awfully mean as regarded Edward; but what could I do? I was in Gaza, gagged and bound; the Philistines hemmed me in.

The same evening the storm burst, the bolt fell, and — to continue the metaphor — the atmosphere grew serene and clear once more. The evening service was shorter than usual, the vicar, as he ascended the pulpit steps, having

dropped two pages out of his sermon-case—
unperceived by any but ourselves, either at the
moment or subsequently when the hiatus was
reached; so, as we joyfully shuffled out I
whispered Edward that by racing home at top
speed we should make time to assume our
bows and arrows (laid aside for the day) and
play at Indians and buffaloes with Aunt Eliza's
fowls—already strolling roostwards, regardless
of their doom—before that sedately-stepping
lady could return. Edward hung at the door,
wavering; the suggestion had unhallowed
charms. At that moment Sabina issued primly
forth, and, seeing Edward, put out her tongue
at him in the most exasperating manner con-
ceivable; then passed on her way, her shoulders
rigid, her dainty head held high. A man can
stand very much in the cause of love: poverty,
aunts, rivals, barriers of every sort, all these
only serve to fan the flame. But personal
ridicule is a shaft that reaches the very vitals.
Edward led the race home at a speed which
one of Ballantyne's heroes might have equalled
but never surpassed; and that evening the
Indians dispersed Aunt Eliza's fowls over
several square miles of country, so that the

tale of them remaineth incomplete unto this day. Edward himself, cheering wildly, pursued the big Cochin-China cock till the bird sank gasping under the drawing-room window, whereat its mistress stood petrified; and after supper, in the shrubbery, smoked a half-consumed cigar he had picked up in the road, and declared to an awe-stricken audience his final, his immitigable resolve to go into the army.

The crisis was past, and Edward was saved! . . . And yet . . . *sunt lachrymæ rerum* . . . to me watching the cigar-stump alternately pale and glow against the dark background of laurel, a vision of a tip-tilted nose, of a small head poised scornfully, seemed to hover on the gathering gloom—seemed to grow and fade and grow again, like the grin of the Cheshire cat—pathetically, reproachfully even; and the charms of the baker's wife slipped from my memory like snow-wreaths in thaw. After all, Sabina was nowise to blame: why should the child be punished? To-morrow I would give them the slip, and stroll round by her garden promiscuous-like, at a time when the farmer was safe in the rick-yard. If nothing came of it, there was no harm done; and if on the contrary. . . . !

THE BURGLARS

IT was much too fine a night to think of going to bed at once, and so, although the witching hour of nine P.M. had struck, Edward and I were still leaning out of the open window in our nightshirts, watching the play of the cedar-branch shadows on the moonlit lawn, and planning schemes of fresh devilry for the sun-shiny morrow. From below, strains of the jocund piano declared that the Olympians were enjoying themselves in their listless impotent way; for the new curate had been bidden to dinner that night, and was at the moment unclerically proclaiming to all the world that he feared no foe. His discordant vociferations doubtless started a train of thought in Edward's mind, for he presently remarked, *à propos* of nothing whatever that had been said before, 'I believe the new curate's rather gone on Aunt Maria.'

I scouted the notion ; 'Why, she's quite old,' I said. (She must have seen some five-and-twenty summers.)

'Of course she is,' replied Edward scornfully. 'It's not her, it's her money he's after, you bet!'

'Didn't know she had any money,' I observed timidly.

'Sure to have,' said my brother with confidence. 'Heaps and heaps.'

Silence ensued, both our minds being busy with the new situation thus presented : mine, in wonderment at this flaw that so often declared itself in enviable natures of fullest endowment,—in a grown-up man and a good cricketer, for instance, even as this curate ; Edward's (apparently) in the consideration of how such a state of things, supposing it existed, could be best turned to his own advantage.

'Bobby Ferris told me,' began Edward in due course, 'that there was a fellow spooning his sister once——'

'What's spooning?' I asked meekly.

'O *I* dunno,' said Edward indifferently. 'It's —it's—it's just a thing they do, you know. And he used to carry notes and messages and things between 'em, and he got a shilling almost every time.'

'What, from each of 'em?' I innocently inquired.

Edward looked at me with scornful pity. 'Girls never have any money,' he briefly explained. 'But she did his exercises, and got him out of rows, and told stories for him when he needed it—and much better ones than he could have made up for himself. Girls are useful in some ways. So he was living in clover, when unfortunately they went and quarrelled about something.'

'Don't see what that's got to do with it,' I said.

'Nor don't I,' rejoined Edward. 'But anyhow the notes and things stopped, and so did the shillings. Bobby was fairly cornered, for he had bought two ferrets on tick, and promised to pay a shilling a week, thinking the shillings were going on for ever, the silly young ass. So when the week was up, and he was being dunned for the shilling, he went off to the fellow and said: "Your broken-hearted Bella implores you to meet her at sundown. By the hollow oak as of old, be it only for a moment.

Do not fail!" He got all that out of some rotten book, of course. The fellow looked puzzled and said:

"What hollow oak? I don't know any hollow oak."

"Perhaps it was the Royal Oak?" said Bobby promptly, 'cos he saw he had made a slip, through trusting too much to the rotten book; but this didn't seem to make the fellow any happier.'

'Should think not,' I said, 'the Royal Oak's an awful low sort of pub.'

'I know,' said Edward. 'Well, at last the fellow said, "I think I know what she means: the hollow tree in your father's paddock. It happens to be an elm, but she wouldn't know the difference. All right: say I'll be there." Bobby hung about a bit, for he hadn't got his money. "She was crying awfully," he said. Then he got his shilling.'

'And wasn't the fellow riled,' I inquired, 'when he got to the place and found nothing?'

'He found Bobby,' said Edward indignantly. 'Young Ferris was a gentleman, every inch of him. He brought the fellow another message from Bella: "I dare not leave the house. My cruel parents immure me closely. If you only knew what I suffer. Your broken-hearted Bella." Out of the same rotten book. This made the fellow a little suspicious, 'cos it was the old Ferrises who had been keen about the thing all through. The fellow, you see, had tin.'

'But what's that got to——' I began again.

'O *I* dunno,' said Edward impatiently. 'I'm telling you just what Bobby told me. He got suspicious, anyhow, but he couldn't exactly call Bella's brother a liar, so Bobby escaped for the time. But when he was in a hole next week, over a stiff French exercise, and tried the same sort of game on his sister, she was too sharp for him, and he got caught out. Somehow women seem more mistrustful than men. They're so beastly suspicious by nature, you know.'

'*I* know,' said I. 'But did the two—the fellow and the sister—make it up afterwards?'

'I don't remember about that,' replied Edward indifferently; 'but Bobby got packed off to school a whole year earlier than his people meant to send him. Which was just what he wanted. So you see it all came right in the end!'

I was trying to puzzle out the moral of this story—it was evidently meant to contain one somewhere—when a flood of golden lamplight mingled with the moon-rays on the lawn, and Aunt Maria and the new curate strolled out on the grass below us, and took the direction of a garden-seat which was backed by a dense laurel shrubbery reaching round in a half-circle to the house. Edward meditated moodily. 'If we only knew what they were talking about,' said he, 'you'd soon see whether I was right or not. Look here! Let's send the kid down by the porch to reconnoitre!'

'Harold's asleep,' I said; 'it seems rather a shame——'

'O rot!' said my brother; 'he's the youngest, and he's got to do as he's told!'

So the luckless Harold was hauled out of bed and given his sailing-orders. He was naturally rather vexed at being stood up suddenly on the cold floor, and the job had no particular interest for him; but he was both staunch and well disciplined. The means of exit were simple enough. A porch of iron trellis came up to within easy reach of the window, and was habitually used by all three

of us, when modestly anxious to avoid public
notice. Harold climbed deftly down the porch
like a white rat, and his night-gown glimmered
a moment on the gravel walk ere he was lost to
sight in the darkness of the shrubbery. A brief
interval of silence ensued; broken suddenly by
a sound of scuffle, and then a shrill long-drawn
squeal, as of metallic surfaces in friction. Our
scout had fallen into the hands of the enemy!

Indolence alone had made us devolve the
task of investigation on our younger brother.
Now that danger had declared itself, there was
no hesitation. In a second we were down the
side of the porch, and crawling Cherokee-wise
through the laurels to the back of the garden-
seat. Piteous was the sight that greeted us.
Aunt Maria was on the seat, in a white evening
frock, looking—for an aunt—really quite nice.
On the lawn stood an incensed curate, grasping
our small brother by a large ear, which—judging from the row he was making—seemed on
the point of parting company with the head it
completed and adorned. The gruesome noise he
was emitting did not really affect us otherwise
than æsthetically. To one who has tried both,
the wail of genuine physical anguish is easily

distinguishable from the pumped-up *ad miseri-cordiam* blubber.   Harold's could clearly be recognised as belonging to the latter class. 'Now you young—' (whelp, *I* think it was, but Edward stoutly maintains it was devil), said the curate sternly; 'tells us what you mean by it!'

'Well leggo of my ear then!' shrilled Harold, 'and I'll tell you the solemn truth!'

'Very well,' agreed the curate, releasing him, 'now go ahead, and don't lie more than you can help.'

We abode the promised disclosure without the least misgiving; but even we had hardly given Harold due credit for his fertility of resource and powers of imagination.

'I had just finished saying my prayers,' began that young gentleman slowly, 'when I happened to look out of the window, and on the lawn I saw a sight which froze the marrow in my veins!   A burglar was approaching the house with snake-like tread!   He had a scowl and a dark lantern, and he was armed to the teeth!'

We listened with interest.   The style, though unlike Harold's native notes, seemed strangely familiar.

'Go on,' said the curate grimly.

'Pausing in his stealthy career,' continued Harold, 'he gave a low whistle. Instantly the signal was responded to, and from the adjacent shadows two more figures glided forth. The miscreants were both armed to the teeth.'

'Excellent,' said the curate ; 'proceed.'

'The robber chief,' pursued Harold, warming to his work, 'joined his nefarious comrades, and conversed with them in silent tones. His expression was truly ferocious, and I ought to have said that he was armed to the t——'

'There, never mind his teeth,' interrupted the curate rudely ; 'there's too much jaw about you altogether. Hurry up and have done.'

'I was in a frightful funk,' continued the narrator, warily guarding his ear with his hand, 'but just then the drawing - room window opened, and you and Aunt Maria came out—I mean emerged. The burglars vanished silently into the laurels, with horrid implications!'

The curate looked slightly puzzled. The tale was well sustained, and certainly circumstantial. After all, the boy might really have seen something. How was the poor man to know—though the chaste and lofty diction

might have supplied a hint—that the whole
yarn was a free adaptation from the last Penny
Dreadful lent us by the knife-and-boot boy?

'Why did you not alarm the house?' he
asked.

''Cos I was afraid,' said Harold sweetly, 'that
p'raps they mightn't believe me!'

'But how did you get down here, you
naughty little boy?' put in Aunt Maria.

Harold was hard pressed—by his own flesh
and blood, too!

At that moment Edward touched me on the
shoulder and glided off through the laurels.
When some ten yards away he gave a low
whistle. I replied with another. The effect was
magical. Aunt Maria started up with a shriek.
Harold gave one startled glance around, and
then fled like a hare, made straight for the
back-door, burst in upon the servants at supper,
and buried himself in the broad bosom of the
cook, his special ally. The curate faced the
laurels—hesitatingly. But Aunt Maria flung
herself on him. 'O Mr. Hodgitts!' I heard
her cry, 'you are brave! for my sake do not be
rash!' He was not rash. When I peeped out
a second later the coast was entirely clear.

By this time there were sounds of a household timidly emerging; and Edward remarked to me that perhaps we had better be off. Retreat was an easy matter. A stunted laurel gave a leg-up on to the garden wall, which led in its turn to the roof of an out-house, up which, at a dubious angle, we could crawl to the window of the box-room. This overland route had been revealed to us one day by the domestic cat, when hard pressed in the course of an otter-hunt, in which the cat—somewhat unwillingly —was filling the title *rôle*; and it had proved distinctly useful on occasions like the present. We were snug in bed—minus some cuticle from knees and elbows—and Harold, sleepily chewing something sticky, had been carried up in the arms of the friendly cook, ere the clamour of the burglar-hunters had died away.

The curate's undaunted demeanour, as reported by Aunt Maria, was generally supposed to have terrified the burglars into flight, and much kudos accrued to him thereby. Some days later, however, when he had dropped in to afternoon tea, and was making a mild curatorial joke about the moral courage required for taking the last piece of bread-and-butter, I felt constrained to remark dreamily, and as it were to the universe at large: 'Mr. Hodgitts! you are brave! for my sake, do not be rash!'

Fortunately for me, the vicar also was a caller on that day; and it was always a comparatively easy matter to dodge my long-coated friend in the open.

A HARVESTING

THE year was in its yellowing time, and the face of Nature a study in old gold. 'A field *or, semée* with garbs of the same:' it may be false Heraldry—Nature's generally is—but it correctly blazons the display that Edward and I considered from the rickyard gate. Harold was not on in this scene, being stretched upon the couch of pain: the special disorder stomachic, as usual. The evening before, Edward, in a fit of unwonted amiability, had deigned to carve me out a turnip lantern, an art-and-craft he was peculiarly deft in; and Harold, as the interior of the turnip flew out in scented fragments under the hollowing knife, had eaten largely thereof: regarding all such jetsam as his special perquisite. Now he was dreeing his weird, with such assistance as the chemist could afford. But Edward and I, knowing that this particular field was to be

carried to-day, were revelling in the privilege
of riding in the empty waggons from the rick-
yard back to the sheaves, whence we returned
toilfully on foot, to career it again over the
billowy acres in these great galleys of a stubble
sea. It was the nearest approach to sailing
that we inland urchins might compass : and
hence it ensued, that such stirring scenes as
Sir Richard Grenville on the *Revenge*, the
smoke-wreathed Battle of the Nile, and the
Death of Nelson, had all been enacted in turn
on these dusty quarter-decks, as they swayed
and bumped afield.

Another waggon had shot its load, and
was jolting out through the rickyard gate, as
we swung ourselves in, shouting, over its tail.
Edward was the first up, and, as I gained
my feet, he clutched me in a death-grapple.
I was a privateersman, he proclaimed, and he
the captain of the British frigate *Terpsichore*,
of — I forget the precise number of guns.
Edward always collared the best parts to himself ; but I was holding my own gallantly,
when I suddenly discovered that the floor
we battled on was swarming with earwigs.
Shrieking, I hurled free of him, and rolled

over the tail-board on to the stubble. Edward
executed a war-dance of triumph on the deck
of the retreating galleon; but I cared little
for that. I knew *he* knew that I wasn't afraid
of him, but that I was—and terribly—of earwigs: 'those mortal bugs o' the field.' So I
let him disappear, shouting lustily for all hands
to repel boarders, while I strolled inland, down
the village.

There was a touch of adventure in the
expedition. This was not our own village,
but a foreign one, distant at least a mile.
One felt that sense of mingled distinction and
insecurity which is familiar to the traveller:
distinction, in that folk turned the head to
note you curiously; insecurity, by reason of the
ever-present possibility of missiles on the part
of the younger inhabitants, a class eternally
Conservative. Elated with isolation, I went
even more nose-in-air than usual: and 'even
so,' I mused, 'might Mungo Park have threaded
the trackless African forest and . . .' Here
I plumped against a soft, but resisting body.

Recalled to my senses by the shock, I fell
back in the attitude every boy under these
circumstances instinctively adopts—both elbows

well up over your ears. I found myself facing
a tall elderly man, clean-shaven, clad in well-
worn black — a clergyman evidently; and I
noted at once a far-away look in his eyes, as
if they were used to another plane of vision,
and could not instantly focus things terrestrial,
being suddenly recalled thereto. His figure was
bent in apologetic protest. 'I ask a thousand pardons, sir,' he said; 'I am really so
very absent-minded. I trust you will forgive
me.'

Now most boys would have suspected chaff
under this courtly style of address. I take
infinite credit to myself for recognising at once
the natural attitude of a man to whom his
fellows were gentlemen all, neither Jew nor
Gentile, clean nor unclean. Of course, I took
the blame on myself; adding, that I was very
absent-minded too. Which was indeed the
case.

'I perceive,' he said pleasantly, 'that we have
something in common. I, an old man, dream
dreams; you, a young one, see visions. Your
lot is the happier. And now—' his hand had
been resting all this time on a wicket-gate—
'you are hot, it is easily seen;—the day is

advanced, *Virgo* is the Zodiacal sign.   Perhaps
I may offer you some poor refreshment, if your
engagements will permit ?'

My only engagement that afternoon was an
arithmetic lesson, and I had not intended to
keep it in any case; so I passed in, while he
held the gate open politely, murmuring '*Venit
Hesperus, ite capellæ* : come, little kid !' and
then apologising abjectly for a familiarity which
(he said) was less his than the Roman poet's.
A straight flagged walk led up to the cool-
looking old house, and my host, lingering in
his progress at this rose-tree and that, forgot
all about me at least twice, waking up and
apologising humbly after each lapse.   During
these intervals I put two and two together,
and identified him as the Rector : a bachelor,
eccentric, learned exceedingly, round whom the
crust of legend was already beginning to form ;
to myself an object of special awe, in that
he was alleged to have written a real book.
'Heaps o' books,' Martha, my informant, said ;
but I knew the exact rate of discount applic-
able to Martha's statements.

We passed eventually through a dark hall
into a room which struck me at once as the

ideal I had dreamed but failed to find. None of your feminine fripperies here! None of your chair-backs and tidies! This man, it was seen, groaned under no aunts. Stout volumes in calf and vellum lined three sides; books sprawled or hunched themselves on chairs and tables; books diffused the pleasant odour of printers' ink and bindings; topping all, a faint aroma of tobacco cheered and heartened exceedingly, as under foreign skies the flap and rustle over the wayfarer's head of the Union Jack—the old flag of emancipation! And in one corner, book-piled like the rest of the furniture, stood a piano.

This I hailed with a squeal of delight. 'Want to strum?' inquired my friend, as if it was the most natural wish in the world— his eyes were already straying towards another corner, where bits of writing-table peeped out from under a sort of Alpine system of book and foolscap.

'O but may I?' I asked in doubt. 'At home I'm not allowed to—only beastly exercises!'

'Well, you can strum here, at all events,' he replied; and murmuring absently, '*Age, dic Latinum, barbite, carmen*,' he made his way, mechanically guided as it seemed, to the irresistible writing-table. In ten seconds he was out of sight and call. A great book open on his knee, another propped up in front, a score or so disposed within easy reach, he read and jotted with an absorption almost passionate. I might have been in Bœotia, for any consciousness he had of me. So with a light heart I turned to and strummed.

Those who painfully and with bleeding feet have scaled the crags of mastery over musical instruments have yet their loss in this : that the wild joy of strumming has become a vanished sense. Their happiness comes from the concord and the relative value of the notes they handle : the pure, absolute quality and nature of each note in itself are only appreciated by the strummer. For some notes have all the sea in them, and some cathedral bells ; others a woodland joyance and a smell of greenery ; in some fauns dance to the merry reed, and even the grave centaurs peep out from their caves. Some bring moonlight, and some the deep crimson of a rose's heart ; some are blue, some red, while others will tell of an army with silken standards and march-music.

And throughout all the sequence of suggestion, up above the little white men leap and peep, and strive against the imprisoning wires; and all the big rosewood box hums as it were full of hiving bees.

Spent with the rapture, I paused a moment and caught my friend's eye over the edge of a folio. 'But as for these Germans,' he began abruptly, as if we had been in the middle of a discussion, 'the scholarship is there, I grant you; but the spark, the fine perception, the happy intuition, where is it? They get it all from us!'

'They get nothing whatever from *us*,' I said decidedly: the word German only suggesting Bands, to which Aunt Eliza was bitterly hostile.

'You think not?' he rejoined doubtfully, getting up and walking about the room. 'Well, I applaud such fairness and temperance in so young a critic. They are qualities—in youth —as rare as they are pleasing. But just look at Schrumpffius, for instance—how he struggles and wrestles with a simple γάρ in this very passage here!'

I peeped fearfully through the open door, half-dreading to see some sinuous and snark-like conflict in progress on the mat; but all

was still. I saw no trouble at all in the passage,
and I said so.

'Precisely,' he cried, delighted. 'To you,
who possess the natural scholar's faculty in so
happy a degree, there is no difficulty at all.
But to this Schrumpffius——' But here, luckily
for me, in came the housekeeper, a clean-look
ing woman of staid aspect.

'Your tea is in the garden,' she said severely,
as if she were correcting a faulty emendation.
'I've put some cakes and things for the little
gentleman; and you'd better drink it before it
gets cold.'

He waved her off and continued his stride,
brandishing an aorist over my devoted head.
The housekeeper waited unmoved till there
fell a moment's break in his descant; and
then, 'You'd better drink it before it gets cold,'
she observed again, impassively. The wretched
man cast a deprecating look at me. 'Perhaps
a little tea would be rather nice,' he observed
feebly; and to my great relief he led the way
into the garden. I looked about for the little
gentleman, but, failing to discover him, I concluded he was absent-minded too, and attacked
the 'cakes and things' with no misgivings.

After a most successful and most learned tea a something happened which, small as I was, never quite shook itself out of my memory. To us at parley in an arbour over the high road, there entered, slouching into view, a dingy tramp, satellited by a frowsy woman and a pariah dog; and, catching sight of us, he set up his professional whine; and I looked at my friend with the heartiest compassion, for I knew well from Martha—it was common talk —that at this time of day he was certainly and surely penniless. Morn by morn he started forth with pockets lined; and each returning evening found him with never a sou. All this he proceeded to explain at length to the tramp, courteously and even shamefacedly, as one who was in the wrong; and at last the gentleman of the road, realising the hopelessness of his case, set to and cursed him with gusto, vocabulary, and abandonment. He reviled his eyes, his features, his limbs, his profession, his relatives and surroundings; and then slouched off, still oozing malice and filth. We watched the party to a turn in the road, where the woman, plainly weary, came to a stop. Her lord, after some conventional expletives demanded of him by his position, relieved her of her bundle, and caused her to hang on his arm with a certain rough kindness of tone, and in action even a dim approach to tenderness; and the dingy dog crept up for one lick at her hand.

'See,' said my friend, bearing somewhat on my shoulder, 'how this strange thing, this love of ours, lives and shines out in the unlikeliest of places! You have been in the fields in early morning? Barren acres, all! But only stoop —catch the light thwartwise—and all is a silver network of gossamer! So the fairy filaments of this strange thing underrun and link together the whole world. Yet it is not the old imperious god of the fatal bow—ἔρως ἀνίκατε μάχαν—not that—nor even the placid respectable στοργή— but something still unnamed, perhaps more mysterious, more divine! Only one must stoop to see it, old fellow, one must stoop!'

The dew was falling, the dusk closing, as I trotted briskly homewards down the road. Lonely spaces everywhere, above and around. Only Hesperus hung in the sky, solitary, pure, ineffably far-drawn and remote; yet infinitely heartening, somehow, in his valorous isolation.

SNOWBOUND

TWELFTH-NIGHT had come and gone, and life next morning seemed a trifle flat and purpose-less. But yester-eve, and the mummers were here! They had come striding into the old kitchen, powdering the red brick floor with snow from their barbaric bedizenments; and stamping, and crossing, and declaiming, till all was whirl and riot and shout. Harold was frankly afraid: unabashed, he buried himself in the cook's ample bosom. Edward feigned a manly superiority to illusion, and greeted these awful apparitions familiarly, as Dick and Harry and Joe. As for me, I was too big to run, too rapt to resist the magic and surprise. Whence came these outlanders, breaking in on us with song and ordered masque and a terrible clashing of wooden swords? And after these, what strange visitants might we not look for any quiet night, when the chestnuts popped in the

ashes, and the old ghost stories drew the awe-
stricken circle close? Old Merlin, perhaps, 'all
furred in black sheep-skins, and a russet gown,
with a bow and arrows, and bearing wild geese
in his hand!' Or stately Ogier the Dane,
recalled from Faëry, asking his way to the land
that once had need of him! Or even, on some
white night, the Snow-Queen herself, with a
chime of sleigh-bells and the patter of reindeer's
feet, halting of a sudden at the door flung wide,
while aloft the Northern Lights went shaking
attendant spears among the quiet stars!

This morning, house-bound by the relentless
indefatigable snow, I was feeling the reaction.
Edward, on the contrary, being violently stage-
struck on this his first introduction to the real
Drama, was striding up and down the floor,
proclaiming 'Here be I, King Gearge the Third,'
in a strong Berkshire accent. Harold, accustomed, as the youngest, to lonely antics and to
sports that asked no sympathy, was absorbed
in 'clubmen': a performance consisting in a
measured progress round the room arm-in-arm
with an imaginary companion of reverend years,
with occasional halts at imaginary clubs, where
—imaginary steps being leisurely ascended—

imaginary papers were glanced at, imaginary
scandal was discussed with elderly shakings of
the head, and—regrettable to say—imaginary
glasses were lifted lipwards.   Heaven only
knows how the germ of this dreary pastime
first found way into his small-boyish being.
It was his own invention, and he was pro-
portionately proud of it.   Meanwhile Charlotte
and I, crouched in the window-seat, watched,
spell-stricken, the whirl and eddy and drive of
the innumerable snow-flakes, wrapping our
cheery little world in an uncanny uniform,
ghastly in line and hue.

Charlotte was sadly out of spirits.   Having
countered' Miss Smedley at breakfast, during
some argument or other, by an apt quotation
from her favourite classic (the *Fairy Book*), she
had been gently but firmly informed that no
such things as fairies ever really existed.   'Do
you mean to say it's all lies?' asked Charlotte
bluntly.   Miss Smedley deprecated the use of
any such unladylike words in any connexion
at all.   'These stories had their origin, my
dear,' she explained, 'in a mistaken anthropo-
morphism in the interpretation of nature.   But
though we are now too well informed to fall

into similar errors, there are still many beautiful
lessons to be learned from these myths——'

'But how can you learn anything,' persisted
Charlotte, 'from what doesn't exist?' And she
left the table defiant, howbeit depressed.

'Don't you mind *her*,' I said consolingly;
'how can she know anything about it? Why,
she can't even throw a stone properly!'

'Edward says they're all rot, too,' replied
Charlotte doubtfully.

'Edward says everything's rot,' I explained,
'now he thinks he's going into the Army. If
a thing's in a book it *must* be true, so that
settles it!'

Charlotte looked almost reassured. The room
was quieter now, for Edward had got the dragon
down and was boring holes in him with a
purring sound; Harold was ascending the
steps of the Athenæum with a jaunty air—
suggestive rather of the Junior Carlton. Outside, the tall elm-tops were hardly to be seen
through the feathery storm. 'The sky's a-
falling,' quoted Charlotte softly; 'I must go
and tell the king.' The quotation suggested a
fairy story, and I offered to read to her, reaching
out for the book. But the Wee Folk were

under a cloud; sceptical hints had embittered
the chalice. So I was fain to fetch *Arthur*—
second favourite with Charlotte for his dames
riding errant, and an easy first with us boys for
his spear-splintering crash of tourney and hurtle
against hopeless odds. Here again, however, I
proved unfortunate; what ill-luck made the
book open at the sorrowful history of Balin
and Balan? 'And he vanished anon,' I read:
'and so he heard an horne blow, as it had been
the death of a beast. " That blast," said Balin,
" is blowen for me, for I am the prize, and yet
am I not dead."' Charlotte began to cry: she
knew the rest too well. I shut the book in
despair. Harold emerged from behind the
arm-chair. He was sucking his thumb (a thing
which members of the Reform are seldom seen
to do), and he stared wide-eyed at his tear-
stained sister. Edward put off his histrionics,
and rushed up to her as the consoler—a new
part for him.

'I know a jolly story,' he began. 'Aunt
Eliza told it me. It was when she was somewhere over in that beastly abroad'—(he had
once spent a black month of misery at Dinan)
—'and there was a fellow there who had got

two storks. And one stork died—it was the she-stork.'—('What did it die of?' put in Harold.)—'And the other stork was quite sorry, and moped, and went on, and got very miserable. So they looked about and found a duck, and introduced it to the stork. The duck was a drake, but the stork didn't mind, and they loved each other and were as jolly as could be. By and by another duck came along —a real she-duck this time—and when the drake saw her he fell in love, and left the stork, and went and proposed to the duck: for she was very beautiful. But the poor stork who was left, he said nothing at all to anybody, but just pined and pined and pined away, till one morning he was found quite dead! But the ducks lived happily ever afterwards!'

This was Edward's idea of a jolly story! Down again went the corners of poor Charlotte's mouth. Really Edward's stupid inability to see the real point in anything was *too* annoying! It was always so. Years before, it being necessary to prepare his youthful mind for a domestic event that might lead to awkward questionings at a time when there was little leisure to invent appropriate answers, it was delicately inquired of him whether he would like to have a little brother, or perhaps a little sister? He considered the matter carefully in all its bearings, and finally declared for a Newfoundland pup. Any boy more 'gleg at the uptak' would have met his parents half-way, and eased their burden. As it was, the matter had to be approached all over again from a fresh standpoint. And now, while Charlotte turned away sniffingly, with a hiccup that told of an overwrought soul, Edward, unconscious (like Sir Isaac's Diamond) of the mischief he had done, wheeled round on Harold with a shout.

'I want a live dragon,' he announced: 'You've got to be my dragon!'

'Leave me go, will you?' squealed Harold, struggling stoutly. 'I'm playin' at something else. How can I be a dragon and belong to all the clubs?'

'But wouldn't you like to be a nice scaly dragon, all green,' said Edward, trying persuasion, 'with a curly tail and red eyes, and breathing real smoke and fire?'

Harold wavered an instant: Pall-Mall was still strong in him. The next he was grovelling on the floor. No saurian ever swung a tail so scaly and so curly as his. Clubland was a thousand years away. With horrific pants he emitted smokiest smoke and fiercest fire.

'Now I want a Princess,' cried Edward, clutching Charlotte ecstatically; 'and *you* can be the Doctor, and heal me from the dragon's deadly wound.'

Of all professions I held the sacred art of healing in worst horror and contempt. Cataclysmal memories of purge and draught crowded thick on me, and with Charlotte—who courted no barren honours—I made a break for the door. Edward did likewise, and the hostile forces clashed together on the mat, and for a brief space things were mixed and chaotic and Arthurian. The silvery sound of the luncheon-bell restored an instant peace, even in the teeth of clenched antagonisms like ours. The Holy Grail itself, 'sliding athwart a sunbeam,' never so effectually stilled a riot of warring passions into sweet and quiet accord.

WHAT THEY TALKED ABOUT

EDWARD was standing ginger-beer like a gentleman, happening, as the one that had last passed under the dentist's hands, to be the capitalist of the flying hour. As in all well-regulated families, the usual tariff obtained in ours: half-a-crown a tooth; one shilling only if the molar were a loose one. This one, unfortunately—in spite of Edward's interested affectation of agony—had been shakiness undisguised; but the event was good enough to run to ginger-beer. As financier, however, Edward had claimed exemption from any servile duties of procurement, and had swaggered about the garden while I fetched from the village post-office, and Harold stole a tumbler from the pantry. Our preparations complete, we were sprawling on the lawn; the staidest and most self-respecting of the rabbits had been let loose to grace the feast, and was lopping demurely about the grass, selecting the juiciest plantains ; while Selina, as the eldest lady present, was toying, in her affected feminine way, with the first full tumbler, daintily fishing for bits of broken cork.

'Hurry up, can't you?' growled our host; 'what are you girls always so beastly particular for?'

'Martha says,' explained Harold (thirsty too, but still just), 'that if you swallow a bit of cork, it swells, and it swells, and it swells inside you, till you——'

'O bosh!' said Edward, draining the glass with a fine pretence of indifference to consequences, but all the same (as I noticed) dodging the floating cork-fragments with skill and judgment.

'O, it's all very well to say bosh,' replied Harold nettled : 'but every one knows it's true but you. Why, when Uncle Thomas was here last, and they got up a bottle of wine for him, he took just one tiny sip out of his glass, and then he said, "Poo, my goodness, that's corked!" And he wouldn't touch it. And they had to get a fresh bottle up. The funny part was, though, I looked in his glass afterwards, when it was brought out into the passage, and there wasn't any cork in it at all! So I drank it all off, and it was very good!'

'You'd better be careful, young man!' said his elder brother, regarding him severely: 'D'you remember that night when the Mummers were here, and they had mulled port, and you went round and emptied all the glasses after they had gone away?'

'Ow! I did feel funny that night,' chuckled Harold. 'Thought the house was comin' down, it jumped about so: and Martha had to carry me up to bed, 'cos the stairs was goin' all waggity!'

We gazed searchingly at our graceless junior; but it was clear that he viewed the matter in the light of a phenomenon rather than of a delinquency.

A third bottle was by this time circling; and Selina, who had evidently waited for it to reach her, took a most unfairly long pull, and then, jumping up and shaking out her frock, announced that she was going for a walk. Then she fled like a hare; for it was the custom of our Family to meet with physical coercion any independence of action in individuals.

'She's off with those Vicarage girls again,' said Edward, regarding Selina's long black legs twinkling down the path. 'She goes out with them every day now; and as soon as ever they start, all their heads go together and they chatter, chatter, chatter the whole blessèd time! I can't make out what they find to talk about. They never stop; it's gabble, gabble, gabble right along, like a nest of young rooks!'

'P'raps they talk about birds'-eggs,' I suggested sleepily (the sun was hot, the turf soft, the ginger-beer potent); 'and about ships, and buffaloes, and desert islands; and why rabbits have white tails; and whether they'd sooner have a schooner or a cutter; and what they'll be when they're men—at least, I mean there's lots of things to talk about, if you *want* to talk.'

'Yes; but they don't talk about those sort of things at all,' persisted Edward. 'How *can* they? They don't *know* anything; they can't *do* anything—except play the piano, and nobody would want to talk about *that*; and they don't care about anything—anything sensible, I mean. So what *do* they talk about?'

'I asked Martha once,' put in Harold; 'and

she said, "Never *you* mind; young ladies has lots of things to talk about that young gentlemen can't understand."'

'I don't believe it,' Edward growled.

'Well, that's what she *said*, anyway,' rejoined Harold indifferently. The subject did not seem to him of first-class importance, and it was hindering the circulation of the ginger-beer.

We heard the click of the front-gate. Through a gap in the hedge we could see the party setting off down the road. Selina was in the middle; a Vicarage girl had her by either arm; their heads were together, as Edward had described; and the clack of their tongues came down the breeze like the busy pipe of starlings on a bright March morning.

'What *do* they talk about, Charlotte?' I inquired, wishing to pacify Edward. 'You go out with them sometimes.'

'I don't know,' said poor Charlotte dolefully. 'They make me walk behind, 'cos they say I'm too little, and mustn't hear. And I *do* want to so,' she added.

'When any lady comes to see Aunt Eliza,' said Harold, 'they both talk at once all the time. And yet each of 'em seems to hear what the other one's saying. I can't make out how they do it. Grown-up people are so clever!'

'The Curate's the funniest man,' I remarked. 'He's always saying things that have no sense in them at all, and then laughing at them as if they were jokes. Yesterday, when they asked him if he'd have some more tea, he said, "Once more unto the breach, dear friends, once more," and then sniggered all over. I didn't see anything funny in that. And then somebody asked him about his button-hole, and he said, "'Tis but a little faded flower," and exploded again. I thought it very stupid.'

'O *him*,' said Edward contemptuously: 'he can't help it, you know; it's a sort of way he's got. But it's these girls I can't make out. If they've anything really sensible to talk about, how is it nobody knows what it is? And if they haven't—and we know they *can't* have, naturally—why don't they shut up their jaw? This old rabbit here—*he* doesn't want to talk. He's got something better to do.' And Edward aimed a ginger-beer cork at the unruffled beast, who never budged.

'O but rabbits *do* talk,' interposed Harold. 'I've watched them often in their hutch. They put their heads together and their noses go up and down, just like Selina's and the Vicarage girls'. Only of course I can't hear what they're saying.'

'Well, if they do,' said Edward unwillingly, 'I'll bet they don't talk such rot as those girls do!' Which was ungenerous, as well as unfair; for it had not yet transpired—nor has it to this day—*what* Selina and her friends talked about.

THE ARGONAUTS

THE advent of strangers, of whatever sort, into our circle had always been a matter of grave dubiety and suspicion. Indeed, it was generally a signal for retreat into caves and fastnesses of the earth, into unthreaded copses or remote outlying cowsheds, whence we were only to be extricated by wily nursemaids, rendered familiar by experience with our secret runs and refuges. It was not surprising, therefore, that the heroes of classic legend, when first we made their acquaintance, failed to win our entire sympathy at once. 'Confidence,' says somebody, 'is a plant of slow growth'; and these stately dark-haired demi-gods, with names hard to master and strange accoutrements, had to win a citadel already strongly garrisoned with a more familiar soldiery. Their chill foreign goddesses had no such direct appeal for us as the mocking malicious fairies and witches of

the North. We missed the pleasant alliance of
the animal—the fox who spread the bushiest of
tails to convey us to the enchanted castle, the
frog in the well, the raven who croaked advice
from the tree ; and—to Harold especially—it
seemed entirely wrong that the hero should ever
be other than the youngest brother of three.
This belief, indeed, in the special fortune that
ever awaited the youngest brother, as such,—
the 'Borough-English' of Faery,—had been of
baleful effect on Harold, producing a certain
self-conceit and perkiness that called for physical
correction. But even in our admonishment we
were on his side ; and as we distrustfully eyed
these new arrivals, old Saturn himself seemed
something of a *parvenu.*

Even strangers, however, if they be good
fellows at heart, may develop into sworn
comrades ; and these gay swordsmen, after all,
were of the right stuff. Perseus, with his cap
of darkness and his wonderful sandals, was
not long in winging his way to our hearts.
Apollo knocked at Admetus' gate in something
of the right fairy fashion. Psyche brought with
her an orthodox palace of magic, as well as
helpful birds and friendly ants. Ulysses, with

his captivating shifts and strategies, broke down the final barrier, and henceforth the band was adopted and admitted into our freemasonry.

I had been engaged in chasing Farmer Larkin's calves—his special pride—round the field, just to show the man we hadn't forgotten him, and was returning through the kitchen-garden with a conscience at peace with all men, when I happened upon Edward, grubbing for worms in the dung-heap. Edward put his worms into his hat, and we strolled along together, discussing high matters of state. As we reached the tool-shed, strange noises arrested our steps; looking in, we perceived Harold, alone, rapt, absorbed, immersed in the special game of the moment. He was squatting in an old pig-trough that had been brought in to be tinkered; and as he rhapsodised, anon he waved a shovel over his head, anon dug it into the ground with the action of those who would urge Canadian canoes. Edward strode in upon him.

'What rot are you playing at now?' he demanded sternly.

Harold flushed up, but stuck to his pig-trough like a man. 'I'm Jason,' he replied defiantly; 'and this is the Argo. The other fellows are here too, only you can't see them; and we're just going through the Hellespont, so don't you come bothering.' And once more he plied the wine-dark sea.

Edward kicked the pig-trough contemptuously. 'Pretty sort of Argo you've got!' said he.

Harold began to get annoyed. ' I can't help it,' he retorted. ' It's the best sort of Argo I can manage, and it's all right if you only pretend enough. But *you* never could pretend one bit.'

Edward reflected. 'Look here,' he said presently.. 'Why shouldn't we get hold of Farmer Larkin's boat, and go right away up the river in a real Argo, and look for Medea, and the Golden Fleece, and everything? And I'll tell you what, I don't mind your being Jason, as you thought of it first.'

Harold tumbled out of the trough in the excess of his emotion. 'But we aren't allowed to go on the water by ourselves,' he cried.

'No,' said Edward, with fine scorn: 'we aren't allowed; and Jason wasn't allowed either, I daresay. But he *went*!'

Harold's protest had been merely conventional: he only wanted to be convinced by sound argument. The next question was, How about the girls? Selina was distinctly handy in a boat: the difficulty about her was, that if she disapproved of the expedition—and, morally considered, it was not exactly a Pilgrim's Progress—she might go and tell; she having just reached that disagreeable age when one begins to develop a conscience. Charlotte, for her part, had a habit of day-dreams, and was as likely as not to fall over-board in one of her rapt musings. To be sure, she would dissolve in tears when she found herself left out; but even that was better than a watery tomb. In fine, the public voice—and rightly, perhaps—was against the admission of the skirted animal: despite the precedent of Atalanta, who was one of the original crew.

'And now,' said Edward, 'who's to ask Farmer Larkin? *I* can't; last time I saw him he said when he caught me again he'd smack my head. *You'll* have to.'

I hesitated, for good reasons. 'You know those precious calves of his?' I began.

Edward understood at once. 'All right,' he said; 'then we won't ask him at all. It doesn't much matter. He'd only be annoyed, and that would be a pity. Now let's set off.'

We made our way down to the stream, and captured the farmer's boat without let or hindrance, the enemy being engaged in the hayfields. This 'river,' so called, could never be discovered by us in any atlas; indeed our Argo could hardly turn in it without risk of shipwreck. But to us 'twas Orinoco, and the cities of the world dotted its shores. We put the Argo's head upstream, since that led away from the Larkin province; Harold was faithfully permitted to be Jason, and we shared the rest of the heroes among us. Then, quitting Thessaly, we threaded the Hellespont with shouts, breathlessly dodged the Clashing Rocks, and coasted under the lee of the Siren-haunted isles. Lemnos was fringed with meadow-sweet, dog-roses dotted the Mysian shore, and the cheery call of the haymaking folk sounded along the coast of Thrace.

After some hour or two's seafaring, the prow of the Argo embedded itself in the mud of a landing-place, plashy with the tread of cows and giving on to a lane that led towards the smoke of human habitations. Edward jumped ashore, alert for exploration, and strode off without waiting to see if we followed; but

I lingered behind, having caught sight of a moss-grown water-gate hard by, leading into a garden that, from the brooding quiet lapping it round, appeared to portend magical possibilities.

Indeed the very air within seemed stiller, as we circumspectly passed through the gate; and Harold hung back shamefaced, as if we were crossing the threshold of some private chamber, and ghosts of old days were hustling past us. Flowers there were, everywhere; but they drooped and sprawled in an overgrowth hinting at indifference; the scent of heliotrope possessed the place as if actually hung in solid festoons from tall untrimmed hedge to hedge. No basket-chairs, shawls, or novels dotted the lawn with colour; and on the garden-front of the house behind, the blinds were mostly drawn. A grey old sun-dial dominated the central sward, and we moved towards it instinctively, as the most human thing in sight. An antick motto ran round it, and with eyes and fingers we struggled at the decipherment.

TIME: TRYETH: TROTHE: spelt out Harold at last. 'I wonder what that means?'

I could not enlighten him, nor meet his further questions as to the inner mechanism of the thing, and where you wound it up. I had seen these instruments before, of course; but had never fully understood their manner of working.

We were still puzzling our heads over the contrivance, when I became aware that Medea herself was moving down the path from the house. Dark-haired, supple, of a figure lightly poised and swayed, but pale and listless—I knew her at once, and having come out to find her, naturally felt no surprise at all. But Harold, who was trying to climb on to the top of the sun-dial, having a cat-like fondness for the summit of things, started and fell prone, barking his chin and filling the pleasance with lamentation.

Medea skimmed the ground swallow-like, and in a moment was on her knees comforting him, wiping the dirt out of his chin with her own dainty handkerchief, and vocal with soft murmur of consolation.

'You needn't take on so about him,' I observed politely. 'He'll cry for just one minute, and then he'll be all right.'

My estimate was justified. At the end of his regulation time Harold stopped crying suddenly, like a clock that had struck its hour; and with a serene and cheerful countenance wriggled out of Medea's embrace, and ran for a stone to throw at an intrusive blackbird.

'O you boys!' cried Medea, throwing wide her arms with abandonment. 'Where have you dropped from? How dirty you are! I've been shut up here for a thousand years, and all that time I've never seen any one under a hundred and fifty! Let's play at something, at once!'

'Rounders is a good game,' I suggested. 'Girls can play at rounders. And we could serve up to the sun-dial here. But you want a bat and a ball, and some more people.'

She struck her hands together tragically. 'I haven't a bat,' she cried, 'or a ball, or more people, or anything sensible whatever. Never mind; let's play at hide-and-seek in the kitchen-garden. And we'll race there, up to that walnut-tree; I haven't run for a century!'

She was so easy a victor, nevertheless, that I began to doubt, as I panted behind, whether she had not exaggerated her age by a year or two. She flung herself into hide-and-seek with all the gusto and abandonment of the true artist; and as she flitted away and reappeared, flushed and laughing divinely, the pale witch-maiden seemed to fall away from her, and she moved rather as that other girl I had read about, snatched from fields of daffodil to reign in shadow below, yet permitted now and again to re-visit earth and light and the frank, caressing air.

Tired at last, we strolled back to the old sun-dial, and Harold, who never relinquished a problem unsolved, began afresh, rubbing his finger along the faint incisions, '*Time tryeth trothe*. Please, I want to know what that means?'

Medea's face drooped low over the sun-dial, till it was almost hidden in her fingers. 'That's what I'm here for,' she said presently in quite a changed, low voice. 'They shut me up here—they think I'll forget—but I never will—never, never! And he, too—but I don't know—it is so long—I don't know!'

Her face was quite hidden now. There was silence again in the old garden. I felt clumsily helpless and awkward. Beyond a vague idea of kicking Harold, nothing remedial seemed to suggest itself.

None of us had noticed the approach of another she-creature—one of the angular and rigid class—how different from our dear comrade! The years Medea had claimed might well have belonged to her; she wore mittens, too—a trick I detested in woman. 'Lucy!' she said sharply, in a tone with *aunt* writ large over it; and Medea started up guiltily.

'You've been crying,' said the newcomer, grimly regarding her through spectacles. 'And pray who are these exceedingly dirty little boys?'

'Friends of mine, aunt,' said Medea promptly, with forced cheerfulness. 'I—I've known them a long time. I asked them to come.'

The aunt sniffed suspiciously. 'You must come indoors, dear,' she said, 'and lie down. The sun will give you a headache. And you little boys had better run away home to your tea. Remember, you should not come to pay visits without your nursemaid.'

Harold had been tugging nervously at my jacket for some time, and I only waited till Medea turned and kissed a white hand to us as she was led away. Then I ran. We gained the boat in safety; and 'What an old dragon!' said Harold.

'Wasn't she a beast!' I replied. 'Fancy the sun giving any one a headache! But Medea was a real brick. Couldn't we carry her off?'

'We could if Edward was here,' said Harold confidently.

The question was, What had become of that defaulting hero? We were not left long in doubt. First, there came down the lane the shrill and wrathful clamour of a female tongue; then Edward, running his best; and then an excited woman hard on his heel. Edward tumbled into the bottom of the boat, gasping 'Shove her off!' And shove her off we did, mightily, while the dame abused us from the bank in the self-same accents in which Alfred hurled defiance at the marauding Dane.

'That was just like a bit out of *Westward Ho!*' I remarked approvingly, as we sculled down the stream. 'But what had you been doing to her?'

'Hadn't been doing anything,' panted Edward, still breathless. 'I went up into the village and explored, and it was a very nice one, and the people were very polite. And there was a blacksmith's forge there, and they were shoeing horses, and the hoofs fizzled and smoked, and smelt so jolly! I stayed there quite a long time. Then I got thirsty, so I asked that old woman for some water, and while she was getting it her cat came out of the cottage, and looked at me in a nasty sort of way, and said something I didn't like. So I went up to it just to—to teach it manners, and somehow or other, next minute it was up an apple-tree, spitting, and I was running down the lane with that old thing after me.'

Edward was so full of his personal injuries that there was no interesting him in Medea at all. Moreover, the evening was closing in, and it was evident that this cutting-out expedition must be kept for another day. As we neared home, it gradually occurred to us that perhaps the greatest danger was yet to come: for the farmer must have missed his boat ere now, and would probably be lying in wait for us near the landing-place. There was no other spot admitting of debarcation on the home side; if we got out on the other, and made for the bridge, we should certainly be seen and cut off. Then it was that I blessed my stars that our elder brother was with us that day. He might be little good at pretending, but in grappling with

the stern facts of life he had no equal.   Enjoin-
ing silence, he waited till we were but a little
way from the fated landing-place, and then
brought us in to the opposite bank.   We
scrambled out noiselessly and—the gathering
darkness favouring us—crouched behind a
willow, while Edward pushed off the empty
boat with his foot.   The old Argo, borne down
by the gentle current, slid and grazed along the
rushy bank ; and when she came opposite the
suspected ambush, a stream of imprecation told
us that our precaution had not been wasted.
We wondered, as we listened, where Farmer
Larkin, who was bucolically bred and reared,
had acquired such range and wealth of vocabulary.   Fully realising at last that his boat was
derelict, abandoned, at the mercy of wind and
wave—as well as out of his reach—he strode
away to the bridge, about a quarter of a mile
further down ; and as soon as we heard his
boots clumping on the planks we nipped out,
recovered the craft, pulled across, and made
the faithful vessel fast to her proper moorings.
Edward was anxious to wait and exchange
courtesies and compliments with the disappointed farmer, when he should confront

us on the opposite bank; but wiser counsels
prevailed. It was possible that the piracy was
not yet laid at our particular door: Ulysses,
I reminded him, had reason to regret a similar
act of bravado, and—were he here—would
certainly advise a timely retreat. Edward held
but a low opinion of me as a counsellor; but he
had a very solid respect for Ulysses.

THE ROMAN ROAD

ALL the roads of our neighbourhood were cheerful and friendly, having each of them pleasant qualities of their own; but this one seemed different from the others in its masterful suggestion of a serious purpose, speeding you along with a strange uplifting of the heart. The others tempted chiefly with their treasures of hedge and ditch; the rapt surprise of the first lords-and-ladies, the rustle of a field-mouse, the splash of a frog; while cool noses of brother-beasts were pushed at you through gate or gap. A loiterer you had need to be, did you choose one of them; so many were the tiny hands thrust out to detain you, from this side and that. But this one was of a sterner sort, and even in its shedding off of bank and hedgerow as it marched straight and full for the open downs, it seemed to declare its contempt for adventitious trappings to catch the shallow-

pated. When the sense of injustice or disappointment was heavy on me, and things were
very black within, as on this particular day, the
road of character was my choice for that solitary
ramble when I turned my back for an afternoon
on a world that had unaccountably declared
itself against me.

'The Knights' Road' we children had named
it, from a sort of feeling that, if from any
quarter at all, it would be down this track we
might some day see Lancelot and his peers
come pacing on their great war-horses; supposing that any of the stout band still survived,
in nooks and unexplored places. Grown-up
people sometimes spoke of it as the 'Pilgrims'
Way'; but I didn't know much about pilgrims
—except Walter in the Horselberg story. Him
I sometimes saw, breaking with haggard eyes
out of yonder copse, and calling to the pilgrims
as they hurried along on their desperate march
to the Holy City, where peace and pardon were
awaiting them. 'All roads lead to Rome,' I
had once heard somebody say; and I had
taken the remark very seriously, of course, and
puzzled over it many days. There must have
been some mistake, I concluded at last; but of

one road at least I intuitively felt it to be true.
And my belief was clinched by something that
fell from Miss Smedley during a history-lesson,
about a strange road that ran right down the
middle of England till it reached the coast, and
then began again in France, just opposite, and
so on undeviating, through city and vineyard,
right from the misty Highlands to the Eternal
City. Uncorroborated, any statement of Miss
Smedley's usually fell on incredulous ears; but
here, with the road itself in evidence, she
seemed, once in a way, to have strayed into
truth.

Rome! It was fascinating to think that it
lay at the other end of this white ribbon that
rolled itself off from my feet over the distant
downs. I was not quite so uninstructed as to
imagine I could reach it that afternoon; but
some day, I thought, if things went on being as
unpleasant as they were now—some day, when
Aunt Eliza had gone on a visit,—some day,
we would see.

I tried to imagine what it would be like when
I got there. The Coliseum I knew, of course,
from a woodcut in the history-book: so to
begin with I plumped that down in the middle.

The rest had to be patched up from the little
grey market-town where twice a year we went
to have our hair cut; hence, in the result,
Vespasian's amphitheatre was approached by
muddy little streets, wherein the Red Lion and
the Blue Boar, with Somebody's Entire along
their front, and 'Commercial Room' on their
windows; the doctor's house, of substantial
red-brick; and the façade of the New Wesleyan
chapel, which we thought very fine, were the
chief architectural ornaments: while the Roman
populace pottered about in smocks and cor-
duroys, twisting the tails of Roman calves and
inviting each other to beer in musical Wessex.
From Rome I drifted on to other cities, faintly
heard of—Damascus, Brighton (Aunt Eliza's
ideal), Athens, and Glasgow, whose glories the
gardener sang; but there was a certain same-
ness in my conception of all of them: that
Wesleyan chapel would keep cropping up
everywhere. It was easier to go a-building
among those dream-cities where no limitations
were imposed, and one was sole architect, with
a free hand. Down a delectable street of cloud-
built palaces I was mentally pacing, when I
happened upon the Artist.

He was seated at work by the roadside, at a point whence the cool large spaces of the downs, juniper-studded, swept grandly westwards. His attributes proclaimed him of the artist tribe: besides, he wore knickerbockers like myself,—a garb confined, I was aware, to boys and artists. I knew I was not to bother him with questions, nor look over his shoulder and breathe in his ear—they didn't like it, this *genus irritabile*. But there was nothing about staring in my code of instructions, the point having somehow been overlooked: so, squatting down on the grass, I devoted myself to the passionate absorbing of every detail. At the end of five minutes there was not a button on him that I could not have passed an examination in; and the wearer himself of that homespun suit was probably less familiar with its pattern and texture than I was. Once he looked up, nodded, half held out his tobacco pouch, mechanically as it were, then, returning it to his pocket, resumed his work, and I my mental photography.

After another five minutes or so had passed, he remarked, without looking my way: 'Fine afternoon we're having: going far to-day?'

'No, I'm not going any farther than this,' I replied; 'I *was* thinking of going on to Rome: but I've put it off.'

'Pleasant place, Rome,' he murmured: 'you'll like it.' It was some minutes later that he added: 'But I wouldn't go just now, if I were you: too jolly hot.'

'*You* haven't been to Rome, have you?' I inquired.

'Rather,' he replied briefly: 'I live there.'

This was too much, and my jaw dropped as I struggled to grasp the fact that I was sitting there talking to a fellow who lived in Rome. Speech was out of the question: besides I had other things to do. Ten solid minutes had I already spent in an examination of him as a mere stranger and artist; and now the whole thing had to be done over again, from the changed point of view. So I began afresh, at the crown of his soft hat, and worked down to his solid British shoes, this time investing everything with the new Roman halo; and at last I managed to get out: 'But you don't really live there, do you?' never doubting the fact, but wanting to hear it repeated.

'Well,' he said, good-naturedly overlooking

the slight rudeness of my query, 'I live there as much as I live anywhere. About half the year sometimes. I've got a sort of a shanty there. You must come and see it some day.'

'But do you live anywhere else as well?' I went on, feeling the forbidden tide of questions surging up within me.

'O yes, all over the place,' was his vague reply. 'And I've got a diggings somewhere off Piccadilly.'

'Where's that?' I inquired.

'Where's what?' said he. 'O, Piccadilly! It's in London.'

'Have you a large garden?' I asked; 'and how many pigs have you got?'

'I've no garden at all,' he replied sadly, 'and they don't allow me to keep pigs, though I'd like to, awfully. It's very hard.'

'But what do you do all day, then,' I cried, 'and where do you go and play, without any garden, or pigs, or things?'

'When I want to play,' he said gravely, 'I have to go and play in the street; but it's poor fun, I grant you. There's a goat, though, not far off, and sometimes I talk to him when I'm feeling lonely; but he's very proud.'

'Goats *are* proud,' I admitted. 'There's one lives near here, and if you say anything to him at all, he hits you in the wind with his head. You know what it feels like when a fellow hits you in the wind?'

'I do, well,' he replied, in a tone of proper melancholy, and painted on.

'And have you been to any other places,' I began again presently, 'besides Rome and Piccy-what's-his-name?'

'Heaps,' he said. 'I'm a sort of Ulysses— seen men and cities, you know. In fact, about the only place I never got to was the Fortunate Island.'

I began to like this man. He answered your questions briefly and to the point, and never tried to be funny. I felt I could be confidential with him.

'Wouldn't you like,' I inquired, 'to find a city without any people in it at all?'

He looked puzzled. 'I'm afraid I don't quite understand,' said he.

'I mean,' I went on eagerly, 'a city where you walk in at the gates, and the shops are all full of beautiful things, and the houses furnished as grand as can be, and there isn't anybody there whatever! And you go into the shops, and take anything you want—chocolates and magic-lanterns and injirubber balls—and there's nothing to pay; and you choose your own house and live there and do just as you like, and never go to bed unless you want to!'

The artist laid down his brush. 'That *would* be a nice city,' he said. 'Better than Rome. You can't do that sort of thing in Rome—or in Piccadilly either. But I fear it's one of the places I've never been to.'

'And you'd ask your friends,' I went on, warming to my subject; 'only those you really like, of course; and they'd each have a house to themselves—there'd be lots of houses,—and there wouldn't be any relations at all, unless they promised they'd be pleasant; and if they weren't they'd have to go.'

'So you wouldn't have any relations?' said the artist. 'Well, perhaps you're right. We have tastes in common, I see.'

'I'd have Harold,' I said reflectively, 'and Charlotte. They'd like it awfully. The others are getting too old. O, and Martha—I'd have Martha to cook and wash up and do things. You'd like Martha. She's ever so much nicer than Aurt Eliza. She's my idea of a real lady.'

'Then I m sure I should like her,' he replied heartily, 'and when I come to—what do you call this city of yours? Nephelo—something, did you say?'

'I—I don't know,' I replied timidly. 'I'm afraid it hasn't got a name—yet.'

The artist gazed out over the downs. '"The poet says, dear city of Cecrops,"' he said softly to himself, '"and wilt not thou say, dear city of Zeus?" That's from Marcus Aurelius,' he went on, turning again to his work. 'You don't know him, I suppose; you will some day.'

'Who's he?' I inquired.

'O, just another fellow who lived in Rome,' he replied, dabbing away.

'O dear!' I cried disconsolately. 'What a lot of people seem to live at Rome, and I've never even been there! But I think I'd like *my* city best.'

'And so would I,' he replied with unction. 'But Marcus Aurelius wouldn't, you know.'

'Then we won't invite him,' I said; 'will we?'

'*I* won't if you won't,' said he. And that point being settled, we were silent for a while.

'Do you know,' he said presently 'I've met one or two fellows from time to time, who have been to a city like yours—perhaps it was the same one. They won't talk much about it— only broken hints, now and then; but they've been there sure enough. They don't seem to care about anything in particular—and everything's the same to them, rough or smooth; and sooner or later they slip off and disappear; and you never see them again. Gone back, I suppose.'

'Of course,' said I. 'Don't see what they ever came away for; *I* wouldn't. To be told you've broken things when you haven't, and stopped having tea with the servants in the kitchen, and not allowed to have a dog to sleep with you. But *I've* known people, too, who've gone there.'

The artist stared, but without incivility.

'Well, there's Lancelot,' I went on. 'The book says he died, but it never seemed to read right, somehow. He just went away, like Arthur. And Crusoe, when he got tired of wearing clothes and being respectable. And all the nice men in the stories who don't marry the Princess, 'cos only one man ever gets married in a book, you know. They'll be there!'

'And the men who never come off,' he said, 'who try like the rest, but get knocked out, or somehow miss—or break down or get bowled over in the mêlée—and get no Princess, nor even a second-class kingdom—some of them'll be there, I hope?'

'Yes, if you like,' I replied, not quite understanding him; 'if they're friends of yours, we'll ask 'em, of course.'

'What a time we shall have!' said the artist reflectively; 'and how shocked old Marcus Aurelius will be!'

The shadows had lengthened uncannily, a tide of golden haze was flooding the grey-green surface of the downs, and the artist began to put his traps together, preparatory to a move. I felt very low: we would have to part, it seemed, just as we were getting on so well together. Then he stood up, and he was very straight and tall, and the sunset was in his hair and beard as he stood there, high over me. He took my hand like an equal. 'I've enjoyed our conversation very much,' he said. 'That was an interesting subject you started, and we haven't

half exhausted it.   We shall meet again, I
hope ?'

'Of course we shall,' I replied, surprised that
there should be any doubt about it.

'In Rome perhaps?' said he.

'Yes, in Rome,' I answered; 'or Piccy-the-
other-place, or somewhere.'

'Or else,' said he, 'in that other city—when
we 've found the way there.   And I 'll look out
for you, and you 'll sing out as soon as you see
me.   And we 'll go down the street arm-in-arm,
and into all the shops, and then I 'll choose my
house, and you 'll choose your house, and we 'll
live there like princes and good fellows.'

'O, but you 'll stay in my house, won't
you?' I cried; 'I wouldn't ask everybody;
but I 'll ask *you*.'

He affected to consider a moment; then
'Right!' he said: 'I believe you mean it, and
I *will* come and stay with you.   I won't go to
anybody else, if they ask me ever so much.
And I 'll stay quite a long time, too, and I
won't be any trouble.'

Upon this compact we parted, and I went
down-heartedly from the man who understood
me, back to the house where I never could do

anything right.   How was it that everything
seemed natural and sensible to him, which these
uncles, vicars, and other grown-up men took
for the merest tomfoolery?   Well, he would
explain this, and many another thing, when
we met again.   The Knights' Road!   How it
always brought consolation!   Was he possibly
one of those vanished knights I had been looking for so long?   Perhaps he would be in
armour next time—why not?   He would look
well in armour, I thought.   And I would take
care to get there first, and see the sunlight flash
and play on his helmet and shield, as he rode
up the High Street of the Golden City.

Meantime, there only remained the finding
it.   An easy matter.

THE SECRET DRAWER

IT must surely have served as a boudoir for the ladies of old time, this little used, rarely entered chamber where the neglected old bureau stood. There was something very feminine in the faint hues of its faded brocades, in the rose and blue of such bits of china as yet remained, and in the delicate old-world fragrance of pot-pourri from the great bowl,—blue and white, with funny holes in its cover,—that stood on the bureau's flat top. Modern aunts disdained this out-of-the-way, backwater, upstairs room, preferring to do their accounts and grapple with their correspondence in some central position more in the whirl of things, whence one eye could be kept on the carriage-drive, while the other was alert for malingering servants and marauding children. Those aunts of a former generation — I sometimes felt — would have suited our habits better. But even by us children, to whom few places were private or reserved, the room was visited but rarely. To be sure, there was nothing particular in it that we coveted or required. Only a few spindle-legged, gilt-backed chairs,—an old harp on which, so the legend ran, Aunt Eliza herself used once to play, in years remote, unchronicled; a corner-cupboard with a few pieces of china; and the old bureau. But one other thing the room possessed, peculiar to itself; a certain sense of privacy — a power of making the intruder feel that he *was* intruding —perhaps even a faculty of hinting that some one might have been sitting on those chairs, writing at the bureau, or fingering the china, just a second before one entered. No such violent word as 'haunted' could possibly apply to this pleasant old-fashioned chamber, which indeed we all rather liked; but there was no doubt it was reserved and stand - offish, keeping itself to itself.

Uncle Thomas was the first to draw my attention to the possibilities of the old bureau. He was pottering about the house one afternoon, having ordered me to keep at his heels for company—he was a man who hated to be left one minute alone,—when his eye fell on it. 'H'm! Sheraton!' he remarked. (He had a smattering of most things, this uncle, especially the vocabularies.) Then he let down the flap, and examined the empty pigeon-holes and dusty panelling. 'Fine bit of inlay,' he went on: 'good work, all of it. I know the sort. There's a secret drawer in there somewhere.' Then as I breathlessly drew near, he suddenly exclaimed: 'By Jove, I do want to smoke!' And, wheeling round, he abruptly fled for the garden, leaving me with the cup dashed from my lips. What a strange thing, I mused, was this smoking, that takes a man suddenly, be he in the court, the camp, or the grove, grips him like an Afreet, and whirls him off to do its imperious behests! Would it be even so with myself, I wondered, in those unknown grown-up years to come?

But I had no time to waste in vain speculations. My whole being was still vibrating to those magic syllables 'secret drawer'; and that particular chord had been touched that never fails to thrill responsive to such words as *cave, trap-door, sliding-panel, bullion, ingots,* or *Spanish dollars.* For, besides its own special bliss, who ever heard of a secret drawer with nothing in it? And O I did want money so badly! I mentally ran over the list of demands which were pressing me the most imperiously.

First, there was the pipe I wanted to give George Jannaway. George, who was Martha's young man, was a shepherd, and a great ally of mine; and the last fair he was at, when he bought his sweetheart fairings, as a right-minded shepherd should, he had purchased a lovely snake expressly for me; one of the wooden sort, with joints, waggling deliciously in the hand; with yellow spots on a green ground, sticky and strong-smelling, as a fresh-painted snake ought to be; and with a red-flannel tongue pasted cunningly into its jaws. I loved it much, and took it to bed with me every night, till what time its spinal cord was loosed and it fell apart, and went the way of all mortal joys. I thought it very nice of George to think of me at the fair, and that's why I wanted to give him a pipe. When the young year was chill and lambing-time was on, George inhabited a little wooden house on wheels, far out on the wintry downs, and saw no faces but such as were sheepish and woolly and mute; and when he and Martha were married, she was going to carry his dinner out to him every day, two miles; and after it, perhaps he would smoke my pipe. It seemed an idyllic sort of existence, for both the parties concerned; but a pipe of quality, a pipe fitted to be part of a life such as this, could not be procured (so Martha informed me) for a smaller sum than eighteenpence. And meantime—— !

Then there was the fourpence I owed Edward; not that he was bothering me for it, but I knew he was in need of it himself, to pay back Selina, who wanted it to make up a sum of two shillings, to buy Harold an ironclad for his approaching birthday, — H.M.S. *Majestic*, now lying uselessly careened in the toyshop window, just when her country had such sore need of her.

And then there was that boy in the village who had caught a young squirrel, and I had never yet possessed one, and he wanted a shilling for it, but I knew that for ninepence in cash— but what was the good of these sorry threadbare reflections? I had wants enough to exhaust any possible find of bullion, even if it amounted to half a sovereign. My only hope now lay in the magic drawer, and here I was, standing and letting the precious minutes slip by! Whether 'findings' of this sort could, morally speaking, be considered 'keepings,' was a point that did not occur to me.

The room was very still as I approached the bureau; possessed, it seemed to be, by a sort of hush of expectation. The faint odour of orris-root that floated forth as I let down the flap, seemed to identify itself with the yellows and browns of the old wood, till hue and scent were of one quality and interchangeable. Even so, ere this, the pot-pourri had mixed itself with the tints of the old brocade, and brocade and pot-pourri had long been one. With expectant fingers I explored the empty pigeon-holes and sounded the depths of the softly-sliding drawers. No books that I knew of gave any general recipe for a quest like this; but the glory, should I succeed unaided, would be all the greater.

To him who is destined to arrive, the fates never fail to afford, on the way, their small encouragements. In less than two minutes, I had come across a rusty button-hook. This was truly magnificent. In the nursery there existed, indeed, a general button-hook, common to either sex ; but none of us possessed a private and special button-hook, to lend or to refuse as suited the high humour of the moment. I pocketed the treasure carefully, and proceeded. At the back of another drawer, three old foreign stamps told me I was surely on the highroad to fortune.

Following on these bracing incentives, came a dull blank period of unrewarded search. In vain I removed all the drawers and felt over every inch of the smooth surfaces, from front to back. Never a knob, spring or projection met the thrilling finger-tips ; unyielding the old bureau stood, stoutly guarding its secret, if secret it really had. I began to grow weary and disheartened. This was not the first time that Uncle Thomas had proved shallow, uninformed, a guide into blind alleys where the echoes mocked you. Was it any good persisting longer ? Was anything any good whatever ? In my mind I began to review past disappointments, and life seemed one long record of failure and of non-arrival. Disillusioned and depressed, I left my work and went to the window. The light was ebbing from the room, and seemed outside to be collecting itself on the horizon for its concentrated effort of sunset. Far down the garden, Uncle Thomas was holding Edward in the air reversed, and smacking him. Edward, gurgling hysterically, was striking blind fists in the direction where he judged his uncle's stomach should rightly be ; the contents of his pockets—a motley show—were strewing the lawn. Somehow, though I had been put through a similar performance myself an hour or two ago, it all seemed very far away and cut off from me.

Westwards the clouds were massing themselves in a low violet bank ; below them, to north and south, as far round as eye could reach, a narrow streak of gold ran out and stretched away, straight along the horizon. Somewhere very far off, a horn was blowing, clear and thin ; it sounded like the golden streak grown audible, while the gold seemed the visible sound. It pricked my ebbing courage, this blended strain of music and colour. I turned for a last effort ; and Fortune thereupon, as if half-ashamed of the unworthy game she had been playing with me, relented, opening her clenched fist. Hardly had I put my hand once more to

the obdurate wood, when with a sort of small
sigh, almost a sob—as it were—of relief, the
secret drawer sprang open.

I drew it out and carried it to the window,
to examine it in the failing light. Too hopeless
had I gradually grown, in my dispiriting search,
to expect very much ; and yet at a glance I saw
that my basket of glass lay in shivers at my
feet. No ingots nor dollars were here, to crown
me the little Monte Cristo of a week. Outside,
the distant horn had ceased its gnat-song, the
gold was paling to primrose, and everything
was lonely and still. Within, my confident
little castles were tumbling down like so many
card-houses, leaving me stripped of estate,
both real and personal, and dominated by the
depressing reaction.

And yet,—as I looked again at the small
collection that lay within that drawer of dis-
illusions, some warmth crept back to my heart
as I recognised that a kindred spirit to my own
had been at the making of it. Two tarnished
gilt buttons—naval, apparently—a portrait of a
monarch unknown to me, cut from some antique
print and deftly coloured by hand in just my
own bold style of brush-work—some foreign

copper coins, thicker and clumsier of make than those I hoarded myself—and a list of birds'-eggs, with names of the places where they had been found. Also, a ferret's muzzle, and a twist of tarry string, still faintly aromatic! It was a real boy's hoard, then, that I had happened upon. He too had found out the secret drawer, this happy-starred young person; and here he had stowed away his treasures, one by one, and had cherished them secretly awhile; and then—what? Well, one would never know now the reason why these priceless possessions still lay here unreclaimed; but across the void stretch of years I seemed to touch hands a moment with my little comrade of seasons—how many seasons?—long since dead.

I restored the drawer, with its contents, to the trusty bureau, and heard the spring click with a certain satisfaction. Some other boy, perhaps, would some day release that spring again. I trusted he would be equally appreciative. As I opened the door to go, I could hear, from the nursery at the end of the passage, shouts and yells, telling that the hunt was up. Bears, apparently, or bandits, were on the evening bill of fare, judging by the character of the noises. In another minute I would be in the thick of it, in all the warmth and light and laughter. And yet—what a long way off it all seemed, both in space and time, to me yet lingering on the threshold of that old-world chamber!

'EXIT TYRANNUS'

THE eventful day had arrived at last, the day which, when first named, had seemed—like all golden dates that promise anything definite—so immeasurably remote. When it was first announced, a fortnight before, that Miss Smedley was really going, the resultant ecstasies had occupied a full week, during which we blindly revelled in the contemplation and discussion of her past tyrannies, crimes, malignities; in recalling to each other this or that insult, dishonour, or physical assault, sullenly endured at a time when deliverance was not even a small star on the horizon: and in mapping out the shining days to come, with special new troubles of their own, no doubt—since this is but a work-a-day world!—but at least free from one familiar scourge. The time that remained had been taken up by the planning of practical expressions of the popular sentiment. Under

Edward's masterly direction, arrangements had
been made for a flag to be run up over the hen-
house at the very moment when the fly, with
Miss Smedley's boxes on top and the grim
oppressor herself inside, began to move off
down the drive.   Three brass cannons, set on
the brow of the sunk-fence, were to proclaim
our deathless sentiments in the ears of the
retreating foe; the dogs were to wear ribbons;
and later—but this depended on our powers of
evasiveness and dissimulation—there might be
a small bonfire, with a cracker or two if the
public funds could bear the unwonted strain.

I was awakened by Harold digging me in
the ribs, and 'She's going to-day!' was the
morning hymn that scattered the clouds of
sleep.   Strange to say, it was with no corre-
sponding jubilation of spirits that I slowly
realised the momentous fact.   Indeed, as I
dressed, a dull disagreeable feeling that I could
not define grew up in me—something like a
physical bruise.   Harold was evidently feeling
it too, for after repeating 'She's going to-day!'
in a tone more befitting the Litany, he looked
hard in my face for direction as to how the
situation was to be taken.   But I crossly bade

him look sharp and say his prayers and not
bother me. What could this gloom portend,
that on a day of days like the present seemed
to hang my heavens with black?

Down at last and out in the sun, we found
Edward before us, swinging on a gate and
chanting a farm-yard ditty in which all the
beasts appear in due order, jargoning in their
several tongues, and every verse begins with
the couplet:

> 'Now my lads, come with me,
> Out in the morning early!'

The fateful exodus of the day had evidently
slipped his memory entirely. I touched him
on the shoulder. 'She's going to-day!' I said.
Edward's carol subsided like a water-tap turned
off. 'So she is!' he replied, and got down at
once off the gate. And we returned to the
house without another word.

At breakfast Miss Smedley behaved in a
most mean and uncalled-for manner. The
right divine of governesses to govern wrong
includes no right to cry. In thus usurping
the prerogative of their victims they ignore
the rules of the ring, and hit below the belt.

Charlotte was crying, of course; but that counted for nothing. Charlotte even cried when the pigs' noses were ringed in due season; thereby evoking the cheery contempt of the operators, who asserted they liked it, and doubtless knew. But when the cloud-compeller, her bolts laid aside, resorted to tears, mutinous humanity had a right to feel aggrieved, and think itself placed in a false and difficult position. What would the Romans have done, supposing Hannibal had cried? History has not even considered the possibility. Rules and precedents should be strictly observed on both sides. When they are violated, the other party is justified in feeling injured.

There were no lessons that morning, naturally —another grievance! The fitness of things required that we should have struggled to the last in a confused medley of moods and tenses, and parted for ever, flushed with hatred, over the dismembered corpse of the multiplication-table. But this thing was not to be; and I was free to stroll by myself through the garden, and combat, as best I might, this growing feeling of depression. It was a wrong system altogether, I thought, this going of people one had got used to. Things ought always to continue as they had been. Change there must be, of course; pigs, for instance, came and went with disturbing frequency—

'Fired their ringing shot and passed,
Hotly charged and sank at last'—

but Nature had ordered it so, and in requital had provided for rapid successors. Did you come to love a pig, and he was taken from you, grief was quickly assuaged in the delight of selection from the new litter. But now, when it was no question of a peerless pig, but only of a governess, Nature seemed helpless, and the future held no litter of oblivion. Things might be better, or they might be worse, but they would never be the same; and the innate conservatism of youth asks neither poverty nor riches, but only immunity from change.

Edward slouched up alongside of me presently, with a hangdog look on him, as if he had been caught stealing jam. 'What a lark it'll be when she's really gone!' he observed, with a swagger obviously assumed.

'Grand fun!' I replied dolorously; and conversation flagged.

We reached the hen-house, and contemplated

the banner of freedom lying ready to flaunt the breezes at the supreme moment.

'Shall you run it up,' I asked, 'when the fly starts, or—or wait a little till it's out of sight?'

Edward gazed round him dubiously. 'We're going to have some rain, I think,' he said; 'and —and it's a new flag. It would be a pity to spoil it. P'raps I won't run it up at all.'

Harold came round the corner like a bison pursued by Indians. 'I've polished up the cannons,' he cried, 'and they look grand! Mayn't I load 'em now?'

'You leave 'em alone,' said Edward severely, 'or you'll be blowing yourself up' (consideration for others was not usually Edward's strong point). 'Don't touch the gunpowder till you're told, or you'll get your head smacked.'

Harold fell behind, limp, squashed, obedient. 'She wants me to write to her,' he began presently. 'Says she doesn't mind the spelling, if I'll only write. Fancy her saying that!'

'O, shut up, will you?' said Edward savagely; and once more we were silent, with only our thoughts for sorry company.

'Let's go off to the copse,' I suggested timidly, feeling that something had to be done to relieve the tension, 'and cut more new bows and arrows.'

'She gave me a knife my last birthday,' said Edward moodily, never budging. 'It wasn't much of a knife—but I wish I hadn't lost it!'

'When my legs used to ache,' I said, 'she sat up half the night, rubbing stuff on them. I forgot all about that till this morning.'

'There's the fly!' cried Harold suddenly. 'I can hear it scrunching on the gravel.'

Then for the first time we turned and stared each other in the face.

*　　*　　*　　*　　*

The fly and its contents had finally disappeared through the gate, the rumble of its wheels had died away. Yet no flag floated defiantly in the sun, no cannons proclaimed the passing of a dynasty. From out the frosted cake of our existence Fate had cut an irreplaceable segment: turn which way we would, the void was present. We sneaked off in different directions, mutually undesirous of company; and it seemed borne in upon me that I ought to go and dig my garden right over, from end to end. It didn't actually want digging; on the other hand no amount of digging could affect it, for good or for evil; so I worked steadily, strenuously, under the hot sun, stifling thought in action. At the end of an hour or so, I was joined by Edward.

'I've been chopping up wood,' he explained, in a guilty sort of way, though nobody had called on him to account for his doings.

'What for?' I inquired stupidly. 'There's piles and piles of it chopped up already.'

'I know,' said Edward, 'but there's no harm in having a bit over. You never can tell what may happen. But what have you been doing all this digging for?'

'You said it was going to rain,' I explained hastily. 'So I thought I'd get the digging done before it came. Good gardeners always tell you that's the right thing to do.'

'It did look like rain at one time,' Edward admitted; 'but it's passed off now. Very queer weather we're having. I suppose that's why I've felt so funny all day.'

'Yes, I suppose it's the weather,' I replied. '*I've* been feeling funny too.'

The weather had nothing to do with it, as we well knew. But we would both have died rather than admit the real reason.

THE BLUE ROOM

THAT nature has her moments of sympathy
with man has been noted often enough,—and
generally as a new discovery. To us, who had
never known any other condition of things, it
seemed entirely right and fitting that the wind
sang and sobbed in the poplar tops, and, in the
lulls of it, sudden spirts of rain spattered the
already dusty roads, on that blusterous March
day when Edward and I awaited, on the station
platform, the arrival of the new tutor. Needless
to say, this arrangement had been planned by
an aunt, from some fond idea that our shy,
innocent young natures would unfold themselves
during the walk from the station, and that, on
the revelation of each other's more solid qualities
that must inevitably ensue, an enduring friendship, springing from mutual respect, might
be firmly based. A pretty dream,—nothing
more. For Edward, who foresaw that the

brunt of tutorial oppression would have to be borne by him, was sulky, monosyllabic, an determined to be as negatively disagreeable as good manners would permit. It was therefore evident that I would have to be spokesman and purveyor of hollow civilities, and I was none the more amiable on that account; all courtesies, welcomes, explanations, and other court-chamberlain kind of business, being my special aversion. There was much of the tempestuous March weather in the hearts of both of us, as we sullenly glowered along the carriage-windows of the slackening train.

One is apt, however, to misjudge the special difficulties of a situation; and the reception proved, after all, an easy and informal matter. In a trainful so uniformly bucolic, a tutor was readily recognisable; and his portmanteau had been consigned to the luggage-cart, and his person conveyed into the lane, before I had discharged one of my carefully considered sentences. I breathed more easily, and looking up at our new friend as we stepped out together, remembered that we had been counting on something altogether more arid, scholastic, and severe. A boyish eager face and a petulant *pince-nez*—untidy hair—a head of constant quick turns like a robin's, and a voice that kept breaking into alto—these were all very strange and new, but not in the least terrible.

He proceeded jerkily through the village, with glances on this side and that; and 'Charming,' he broke out presently; 'quite too charming and delightful!'

I had not counted on this sort of thing, and glanced for help to Edward, who, hands in pockets, looked grimly down his nose. He had taken his line, and meant to stick to it.

Meantime our friend had made an imaginary spy-glass out of his fist, and was squinting through it at something I could not perceive. 'What an exquisite bit!' he burst out. 'Fifteenth century—no—yes it is!'

I began to feel puzzled, not to say alarmed. It reminded me of the butcher in the *Arabian Nights*, whose common joints, displayed on the shop-front, took to a startled public the appearance of dismembered humanity. This man seemed to see the strangest things in our dull, familiar surroundings.

'Ah!' he broke out again, as we jogged on between hedgerows: 'and that field now—backed by the downs—with the rain-cloud brooding over it,—that's all David Cox—every bit of it!'

'That field belongs to Farmer Larkin,' I explained politely; for of course he could not be expected to know. 'I'll take you over to Farmer Cox's to-morrow, if he's a friend of yours; but there's nothing to see there.'

Edward, who was hanging sullenly behind, made a face at me, as if to say, 'What sort of lunatic have we got here?'

'It has the true pastoral character, this country of yours,' went on our enthusiast: 'with just that added touch in cottage and farmstead, relics of a bygone art, which makes our English landscape so divine, so unique!'

Really this grasshopper was becoming a burden! These familiar fields and farms, of which we knew every blade and stick, had done nothing that I knew of to be bespattered with adjectives in this way. I had never thought of them as divine, unique, or anything else. They were—well, they were just themselves, and there was an end of it. Despairingly I jogged Edward in the ribs, as a sign to start rational conversation, but he only grinned and continued obdurate.

'You can see the house now,' I remarked presently; 'and that's Selina, chasing the donkey in the paddock. Or is it the donkey chasing Selina? I can't quite make out; but it's *them*, anyhow.'

Needless to say, he exploded with a full charge of adjectives. 'Exquisite!' he rapped out; 'so mellow and harmonious! and so entirely in keeping!' (I could see from Edward's face that he was thinking who ought to be in keeping.) 'Such possibilities of romance, now, in those old gables!'

'If you mean the garrets,' I said, 'there's a lot of old furniture in them; and one is generally full of apples; and the bats get in sometimes, under the eaves, and flop about till we go up with hair-brushes and things and drive 'em out; but there's nothing else in them that I know of.'

'O, but there must be more than bats,' he cried. 'Don't tell me there are no ghosts. I shall be deeply disappointed if there aren't any ghosts.'

I did not think it worth while to reply, feeling really unequal to this sort of conversation. Besides, we were nearing the house, when my task would be ended. Aunt Eliza met us at the door, and in the cross-fire of adjectives that ensued — both of them talking at once, as grown-up folk have a habit of doing—we two slipped round to the back of the house, and speedily put several broad acres between us and civilisation, for fear of being ordered in to tea in the drawing-room. By the time we returned, our new importation had gone up to dress for dinner, so till the morrow at least we were free of him.

Meanwhile the March wind, after dropping a while at sundown, had been steadily increasing in volume ; and although I fell asleep at my usual hour, about midnight I was wakened by the stress and the cry of it. In the bright moon-light, wind-swung branches tossed and swayed eerily across the blinds ; there was rumbling in chimneys, whistling in keyholes, and every-where a clamour and a call. Sleep was out of the question, and, sitting up in bed, I looked round. Edward sat up too. 'I was wondering when you were going to wake,' he said. 'It's no good trying to sleep through this. I vote we get up and do something.'

'I'm game,' I replied. 'Let's play at being in a ship at sea' (the plaint of the old house under the buffeting wind suggested this, naturally); 'and we can be wrecked on an island, or left on a raft, whichever you choose; but I like an island best myself, because there's more things on it.'

Edward on reflection negatived the idea. 'It would make too much noise,' he pointed out. 'There's no fun playing at ships, unless you can make a jolly good row.'

The door creaked, and a small figure in white slipped cautiously in. 'Thought I heard you talking,' said Charlotte. 'We don't like it; we're afraid—Selina too! She'll be here in a minute. She's putting on her new dressing-gown she's so proud of.'

His arms round his knees, Edward cogitated deeply until Selina appeared, barefooted, and looking slim and tall in the new dressing-gown. Then, 'Look here,' he exclaimed; 'now we're all together, I vote we go and explore!'

'You're always wanting to explore,' I said. 'What on earth is there to explore for in this house?'

'Biscuits!' said the inspired Edward.

'Hooray! Come on!' chimed in Harold, sitting up suddenly. He had been awake all the time, but had been shamming asleep, lest he should be fagged to do anything.

It was indeed a fact, as Edward had remembered, that our thoughtless elders occasionally left the biscuits out, a prize for the night-walking adventurer with nerves of steel.

Edward tumbled out of bed, and pulled a baggy old pair of knickerbockers over his bare shanks.   Then he girt himself with a belt, into which he thrust, on the one side a large wooden pistol, on the other an old single-stick; and finally he donned a big slouch-hat—once an uncle's—that we used for playing Guy Fawkes and Charles-the-Second-up-a-tree in.   Whatever the audience, Edward, if possible, always dressed for his parts with care and conscientiousness; while Harold and I, true Elizabethans, cared little about the mounting of the piece, so long as the real dramatic heart of it beat sound.

Our commander now enjoined on us a silence deep as the grave, reminding us that Aunt Eliza usually slept with an open door, past which we had to file.

'But we'll take the short cut through the Blue Room,' said the wary Selina.

'Of course,' said Edward approvingly. 'I forgot about that. Now then! You lead the way!'

The Blue Room had in prehistoric times been added to by taking in a superfluous passage, and so not only had the advantage of two doors, but also enabled us to get to the head of the stairs without passing the chamber wherein our dragon-aunt lay couched. It was rarely occupied, except when a casual uncle came down for the night. We entered in noiseless file, the room being plunged in darkness, except for a bright strip of moonlight on the floor, across which we must pass for our exit. On this our leading lady chose to pause, seizing the opportunity to study the hang of her new dressing-gown. Greatly satisfied thereat, she proceeded, after the feminine fashion, to peacock and to pose, pacing a minuet down the moonlit patch with an imaginary partner. This was too much for Edward's histrionic instincts, and after a moment's pause he drew his single-stick, and, with flourishes meet for the occasion, strode on to the stage. A struggle ensued on approved lines, at the end of which Selina was stabbed slowly and with unction, and her corpse borne from the chamber by the ruthless cavalier.

The rest of us rushed after in a clump, with capers and gesticulations of delight; the special charm of the performance lying in the necessity for its being carried out with the dumbest of dumb shows.

Once out on the dark landing, the noise of the storm without told us that we had exaggerated the necessity for silence; so, grasping the tails of each other's nightgowns, even as Alpine climbers rope themselves together in perilous places, we fared stoutly down the staircase-moraine, and across the grim glacier of the hall, to where a faint glimmer from the half-open door of the drawing-room beckoned to us like friendly hostel-lights. Entering, we found that our thriftless seniors had left the sound red heart of a fire, easily coaxed into a cheerful blaze; and biscuits—a plateful—smiled at us in an encouraging sort of way, together with the halves of a lemon, already squeezed, but still suckable. The biscuits were righteously shared, the lemon segments passed from mouth to mouth; and as we squatted round the fire, its genial warmth consoling our unclad limbs, we realised that so many nocturnal perils had not been braved in vain.

'It's a funny thing,' said Edward, as we chatted, 'how I hate this room in the daytime. It always means having your face washed, and your hair brushed, and talking silly company talk. But to - night it's really quite jolly. Looks different, somehow.'

'I never can make out,' I said, 'what people come here to tea for. They can have their own tea at home if they like—they're not poor people—with jam and things, and drink out of their saucer, and suck their fingers and enjoy themselves; but they come here from a long way off, and sit up straight with their feet off the bars of their chairs, and have one cup, and talk the same sort of stuff every time.'

Selina sniffed disdainfully. 'You don't know anything about it,' she said. 'In society you have to call on each other. It's the proper thing to do.'

'Pooh! *you're* not in society,' said Edward politely; 'and, what's more, you never will be.'

'Yes I shall, some day,' retorted Selina; 'but I shan't ask you to come and see me, so there!'

'Wouldn't come if you did,' growled Edward.

'Well you won't get the chance,' rejoined

our sister, claiming her right of the last word.
There was no heat about these little amenities,
which made up—as understood by us—the art
of polite conversation.

'I don't like society people,' put in Harold
from the sofa, where he was sprawling at full
length—a sight the daylight hours would have
blushed to witness. 'There were some of 'em
here this afternoon, when you two had gone off
to the station. O, and I found a dead mouse
on the lawn, and I wanted to skin it, but I
wasn't sure I knew how, by myself; and they
came out into the garden, and patted my head
—I wish people wouldn't do that—and one of
em asked me to pick her a flower. Don't
know why she couldn't pick it herself; but I
said, 'All right, I will if you'll hold my mouse.'
But she screamed, and threw it away; and
Augustus (the cat) got it, and ran away with it.
I believe it was really his mouse all the time,
'cos he'd been looking about as if he had lost
something, so I wasn't angry with *him*. But
what did *she* want to throw away my mouse
for?'

'You have to be careful with mice,' reflected
Edward; 'they're such slippery things. Do you

remember we were playing with a dead mouse once on the piano, and the mouse was Robinson Crusoe, and the piano was the island, and somehow Crusoe slipped down inside the island, into its works, and we couldn't get him out, though we tried rakes and all sorts of things, till the tuner came. And that wasn't till a week after, and then——'

Here Charlotte who had been nodding solemnly, fell over into the fender; and we realised that the wind had dropped at last, and the house was lapped in a great stillness. Our vacant beds seemed to be calling to us imperiously; and we were all glad when Edward gave the signal for retreat. At the top of the staircase Harold unexpectedly turned mutinous, insisting on his right to slide down the banisters in a free country. Circumstances did not allow of argument; I suggested frog's-marching instead, and accordingly frog's-marched he was, the procession passing solemnly across the moon-lit Blue Room, with Harold horizontal and limply submissive. Snug in bed at last, I was just slipping off into slumber when I heard Edward explode, with chuckle and snort.

'By Jove!' he said; 'I forgot all about

it. The new tutor's sleeping in the Blue
Room!'

'Lucky he didn't wake up and catch us,' I
grunted drowsily; and, without another thought
on the matter, we both sank into well-earned
repose.

Next morning, coming down to breakfast
braced to grapple with fresh adversity, we were
surprised to find our garrulous friend of the
previous day — he was late in making his
appearance—strangely silent and (apparently)
pre-occupied. Having polished off our porridge,
we ran out to feed the rabbits, explaining to
them that a beast of a tutor would prevent
their enjoying so much of our society as
formerly.

On returning to the house at the fated hour
appointed for study, we were thunderstruck to
see the station-cart disappearing down the
drive, freighted with our new acquaintance.
Aunt Eliza was brutally uncommunicative;
but she was overheard to remark casually that
she thought the man must be a lunatic. In
this theory we were only too ready to concur,
dismissing thereafter the whole matter from our
minds.

Some weeks later it happened that Uncle Thomas, while paying us a flying visit, produced from his pocket a copy of the latest weekly, *Psyche: a Journal of the Unseen*; and proceeded laboriously to rid himself of much incomprehensible humour, apparently at our expense. We bore it patiently, with the forced grin demanded by convention, anxious to get at the source of inspiration, which it presently appeared lay in a paragraph circumstantially describing our modest and humdrum habitation. 'Case III.,' it began. 'The following particulars were communicated by a young member of the Society, of undoubted probity and earnestness, and are a chronicle of actual and recent experience.' A fairly accurate description of the house followed, with details that were unmistakable; but to this there succeeded a flood of meaningless drivel about apparitions, nightly visitants, and the like, writ in a manner betokening a disordered mind, coupled with a feeble imagination. The fellow was not even original. All the old material was there—the storm at night, the haunted chamber, the white lady, the murder re-enacted, and so on—already worn threadbare in many a Christmas Number.

No one was able to make head or tail of the stuff, or of its connexion with our quiet mansion; and yet Edward, who had always suspected the fellow, persisted in maintaining that our tutor of a brief span was, somehow or other, at the bottom of it.

A FALLING OUT

HAROLD told me the main facts of this episode some time later,—in bits and with reluctance. It was not a recollection he cared to talk about. The crude blank misery of a moment is apt to leave a dull bruise which is slow to depart, if it ever do so entirely; and Harold confesses to a twinge or two, still, at times, like the veteran who brings home a bullet inside him from martial plains over sea.

He knew he was a brute the moment he had done it. Selina had not meant to worry, only to comfort and assist. But his soul was one raw sore within him, when he found himself shut up in the schoolroom after hours, merely for insisting that 7 times 7 amounted to 47. The injustice of it seemed so flagrant. Why not 47 as much as 49? One number was no

prettier than the other to look at, and it was
evidently only a matter of arbitrary taste and
preference, and, anyhow, it had always been
47 to him, and would be to the end of time.
So when Selina came in out of the sun, leaving
the Trappers of the Far West behind her, and
putting off the glory of being an Apache squaw
in order to hear him his tables and win his
release, Harold turned on her venomously, rejected her kindly overtures, and even drove his
elbow into her sympathetic ribs, in his deter-
mination to be left alone in the glory of sulks.
The fit passed directly, his eyes were opened,
and his soul sat in the dust as he sorrowfully
began to cast about for some atonement heroic
enough to salve the wrong.

Of course poor Selina looked for no sacrifice
nor heroics whatever; she didn't even want him
to say he was sorry. If he would only make it
up, she would have done the apologising part
herself. But that was not a boy's way. Something solid, Harold felt, was due from him; and
until that was achieved, making-up must not
be thought of, in order that the final effect
might not be spoilt. Accordingly, when his
release came, and Selina hung about trying to

catch his eye, Harold, possessed by the demon of a distorted motive, avoided her steadily— though he was bleeding inwardly at every minute of delay — and came to me instead. Needless to say, I warmly approved his plan. It was so much more high-toned than just going and making-up tamely, which any one could do; and a girl who had been jobbed in the ribs by a hostile elbow could not be expected for a moment to overlook it, without the liniment of an offering to soothe her injured feelings.

'I know what she wants most,' said Harold. 'She wants that set of tea-things in the toy-shop window, with the red and blue flowers on 'em; she's wanted it for months, 'cos her dolls are getting big enough to have real afternoon tea; and she wants it so badly that she won't walk that side of the street when we go into the town. But it costs five shillings!'

Then we set to work seriously, and devoted the afternoon to a realisation of assets and the composition of a Budget that might have been dated without shame from Whitehall. The result worked out as follows :—

	s.	d
By one uncle, unspent through having been lost for nearly a week—turned up at last in the straw of the dog-kennel . .	2	6
By advance from me on security of next uncle, and failing that, to be called in at Christmas	1	0
By shaken out of missionary-box with the help of a knife-blade. (They were our own pennies and a forced levy) . .	0	4
By bet due from Edward, for walking across the field where Farmer Larkin's bull was, and Edward bet him twopence he wouldn't—called in with difficulty . .	0	2
By advance from Martha, on no security at all, only you mustn't tell your aunt . .	1	0
Total	5	0

and at last we breathed again.

The rest promised to be easy. Selina had a tea-party at five on the morrow, with the chipped old wooden tea-things that had served her successive dolls from babyhood. Harold would slip off directly after dinner, going alone, so as not to arouse suspicion, as we were not allowed to go into the town by ourselves. It was nearly two miles to our small metropolis, but there would be plenty of time for him to go and return, even laden with the olive-branch neatly packed in shavings. Besides, he might meet the butcher, who was his friend and would give him

a lift. Then, finally, at five, the rapture of the
new tea-service, descended from the skies; and,
retribution made, making-up at last, without
loss of dignity. With the event before us, we
thought it a small thing that twenty-four hours
more of alienation and pretended sulks must
be kept up on Harold's part; but Selina, who
naturally knew nothing of the treat in store for
her, moped for the rest of the evening, and took
a very heavy heart to bed.

Next day when the hour for action arrived,
Harold evaded Olympian attention with an
easy modesty born of long practice, and made
off for the front gate. Selina, who had been
keeping her eye upon him, thought he was
going down to the pond to catch frogs, a joy
they had planned to share together, and made
after him. But Harold, though he heard her
footsteps, continued sternly on his high mission,
without even looking back; and Selina was left
to wander disconsolately among flower-beds that
had lost—for her—all scent and colour. I saw
it all, and, although cold reason approved our
line of action, instinct told me we were brutes.

Harold reached the town—so he recounted
afterwards—in record time, having run most

of the way for fear the tea-things, which had reposed six months in the window, should be snapped up by some other conscience-stricken lacerator of a sister's feelings; and it seemed hardly credible to find them still there, and their owner willing to part with them for the price marked on the ticket. He paid his money down at once, that there should be no drawing back from the bargain; and then, as the things had to be taken out of the window and packed, and the afternoon was yet young, he thought he might treat himself to a taste of urban joys and the *vie de Bohême*. Shops came first, of course, and he flattened his nose successively against the window with the indiarubber balls in it, and the clock-work locomotive; and against the barber's window, with wigs on blocks, reminding him of uncles, and shaving-cream that looked so good to eat; and the grocer's window, displaying more currants than the whole British population could possibly consume without a special effort; and the window of the bank, wherein gold was thought so little of that it was dealt about in shovels. Next there was the market-place, with all its clamorous joys; and when a runaway calf came

down the street like a cannon-ball, Harold felt
that he had not lived in vain. The whole place
was so brimful of excitement that he had quite
forgotten the why and the wherefore of his
being there, when a sight of the church clock
recalled him to his better self, and sent him
flying out of the town, as he realised he had
only just time enough left to get back in. If
he were after his appointed hour, he would not
only miss his high triumph, but probably would
be detected as a transgressor of bounds—a
crime before which a private opinion on multi-
plication sank to nothingness. So he jogged
along on his homeward way, thinking of many
things, and probably talking to himself a good
deal, as his habit was. He had covered nearly
half the distance, when suddenly—a deadly
sinking in the pit of his stomach—a paralysis
of every limb—around him a world extinct of
light and music—a black sun and a reeling
sky—he had forgotten the tea-things!

It was useless, it was hopeless, all was over,
and nothing could now be done. Nevertheless
he turned and ran back wildly, blindly, choking
with the big sobs that evoked neither pity nor
comfort from a merciless mocking world around;

a stitch in his side, dust in his eyes, and black
despair clutching at his heart. So he stumbled
on, with leaden legs and bursting sides, till—as
if Fate had not yet dealt him her last worst
buffet of all—on turning a corner in the road
he almost ran under the wheels of a dog-cart,
in which, as it pulled up, was apparent the
portly form of Farmer Larkin, the arch-enemy,
at whose ducks he had been shying stones that
very morning!

Had Harold been in his right and unclouded
senses, he would have vanished through the
hedge some seconds earlier, rather than pain
the farmer, by any unpleasant reminiscences
which his appearance might recall; but, as
things were, he could only stand and blubber
hopelessly, caring, indeed, little now what
further misery might befall him. The farmer,
for his part, surveyed the desolate figure with
some astonishment, calling out in no unfriendly
accents, 'Why, Master Harold! whatever be
the matter? Baint runnin' away, be ee?'

Then Harold, with the unnatural courage
born of desperation, flung himself on the step,
and, climbing into the cart, fell in the straw at
the bottom of it, sobbing out that he wanted to

go back, go back! The situation had a vague-
ness; but the farmer, a man of action rather
than of words, swung his horse round smartly,
and they were in the town again by the time
Harold had recovered himself sufficiently to
furnish details. As they drove up to the shop,
the woman was waiting at the door with the
parcel; and hardly a minute seemed to have
elapsed since the black crisis, ere they were
bowling along swiftly home, the precious parcel
hugged in a close embrace.

And now the farmer came out in quite a new
and unexpected light. Never a word did he
say of broken fences and hurdles, of trampled
crops and harried flocks and herds. One would
have thought the man had never possessed a
head of live stock in his life. Instead, he was
deeply interested in the whole dolorous quest
of the tea-things, and sympathised with Harold
on the disputed point in mathematics as if he
had been himself at the same stage of educa-
tion. As they neared home, Harold found
himself, to his surprise, sitting up and chatting
to his new friend like man to man; and before
he was set down at a convenient gap in the
garden hedge, he had promised that when

Selina gave her first public tea-party, little Miss Larkin should be invited to come and bring her whole sawdust family along with her; and the farmer appeared as pleased and proud as if he had won a gold medal at the Agricultural Show, and really, when I heard the story, it began to dawn upon me that those Olympians must have certain good points, far down in them, and that I should have to leave off abusing them some day.

At the hour of five, Selina, having spent the afternoon searching for Harold in all his accustomed haunts, sat down disconsolately to tea with her dolls, who ungenerously refused to wait beyond the appointed hour. The wooden tea-things seemed more chipped than usual; and the dolls themselves had more of wax and sawdust, and less of human colour and intelligence about them, than she ever remembered before. It was then that Harold burst in, very dusty, his stockings at his heels, and the channels ploughed by tears still showing on his grimy cheeks; and Selina was at last permitted to know that he had been thinking of her ever since his ill-judged exhibition of temper, and that his sulks had not been the genuine article, nor had he gone frogging by himself. It was a very happy hostess who dispensed hospitality that evening to a glassy-eyed stiff-kneed circle; and many a dollish *gaucherie*, that would have been severely checked on ordinary occasions, was as much overlooked as if it had been a birthday.

But Harold and I, in what I was afterwards given to understand was our stupid masculine way, thought all her happiness sprang from possession of the long-coveted tea-service.

'LUSISTI SATIS'

AMONG the many fatuous ideas that possessed the Olympian noddle, this one was pre-eminent; that, being Olympians, they could talk quite freely in our presence on subjects of the closest import to us, so long as names, dates, and other landmarks were ignored. We were supposed to be denied the faculty for putting two and two together; and like the monkeys, who very sensibly refrain from speech lest they should be set to earn their livings, we were careful to conceal our capabilities for a simple syllogism. Thus we were rarely taken by surprise, and so were considered by our disappointed elders to be apathetic and to lack the divine capacity for wonder.

Now the daily output of the letter-bag, with the mysterious discussions that ensued thereon, had speedily informed us that Uncle Thomas was intrusted with a mission—a mission, too, affecting ourselves. Uncle Thomas's missions were many and various. A self-important man, one liking the business while protesting that he sank under the burden, he was the missionary, so to speak, of our remote habitation. The matching a ribbon, the running down to the stores, the interviewing a cook — these and similar duties lent constant colour and variety to his vacant life in London, and helped to keep down his figure. When the matter, however, had in our presence to be referred to with nods and pronouns, with significant hiatuses and interpolations in the French tongue, then the red flag was flown, the storm-cone hoisted, and by a studious pretence of inattention we were not long in plucking out the heart of the mystery.

To clinch our conclusion, we descended suddenly and together on Martha; proceeding, however, not by simple inquiry as to facts— that would never have done; but by informing her that the air was full of school and that we knew all about it, and then challenging denial. Martha was a trusty soul, but a bad witness for the defence, and we soon had it all out of her. The word had gone forth, the school had been selected; the necessary sheets were hemming even now, and Edward was the designated and appointed victim.

It had always been before us as an inevitable bourne, this strange unknown thing called school; and yet—perhaps I should say consequently—we had never seriously set ourselves to consider what it really meant. But now that the grim spectre loomed imminent, stretching lean hands for one of our flock, it behoved us to face the situation, to take soundings in this uncharted sea and find out whither we were drifting. Unfortunately the data in our possession were absolutely insufficient, and we knew not whither to turn for exact information. Uncle Thomas could have told us all about it, of course; he had been there himself, once, in the dim and misty past. But an unfortunate conviction, that nature had intended him for a humorist, tainted all his evidence, besides making it wearisome to hear. Again, of such among our contemporaries as we had approached, the trumpets gave forth an uncertain sound. According to some it meant larks, revels, emancipation, and a foretaste of the bliss of manhood. According to others—the majority, alas!—it was a private and peculiar Hades, that could give the original institution points and a beating. When Edward was observed to be swaggering round with a jaunty air and his chest stuck out, I knew that he was contemplating his future from the one point of view. When, on the contrary, he was subdued and unaggressive, and sought the society of his sisters, I recognised that the other aspect was in the ascendant. 'You can always run away, you know,' I used to remark consolingly on these latter occasions; and Edward would brighten up wonderfully at the suggestion, while Charlotte melted into tears before her vision of a brother with blistered feet and an empty belly, passing nights of frost 'neath the lee of windy haystacks.

It was to Edward, of course, that the situation was chiefly productive of anxiety; and yet the ensuing change in my own circumstances and position furnished me also with food for grave reflexion. Hitherto I had acted mostly to orders. Even when I had devised and counselled any particular devilry, it had been carried out on Edward's approbation, and—as eldest— at his special risk. Henceforward I began to

be anxious of the bugbear Responsibility, and
to realise what a soul-throttling thing it is.
True, my new position would have its com-
pensations.   Edward had been masterful exceedingly, imperious, perhaps a little narrow;
impassioned for hard facts, and with scant sympathy for make-believe.   I should now be free
and untrammelled ; in the conception and the
carrying out of a scheme, I could accept and
reject to better artistic purpose.

It would, moreover, be needless to be a
Radical any more.   Radical I never was, really,
by nature or by sympathy.   The part had been
thrust on me one day, when Edward proposed
to foist the House of Lords on our small
republic.   The principles of the thing he set
forth learnedly and well, and it all sounded
promising enough, till he went on to explain
that, for the present at least, he proposed to be
the House of Lords himself.   We others were
to be the Commons.   There would be promotions,
of course, he added, dependent on service and
on fitness, and open to both sexes ; and to me
in especial he held out hopes of speedy advance-
ment.   But in its initial stages the thing wouldn't
work properly unless he were first and only

Lord. Then I put my foot down promptly, and said it was all rot, and I didn't see the good of any House of Lords at all. 'Then you must be a Low Radical!' said Edward, with fine contempt. The inference seemed hardly necessary, but what could I do? I accepted the situation, and said firmly, Yes, I was a low Radical. In this monstrous character I had been obliged to masquerade ever since; but now I could throw it off, and look the world in the face again.

And yet, did this and other gains really outbalance my losses? Henceforth I should it was true, be leader and chief; but I should also be the buffer between the Olympians and my little clan. To Edward this had been nothing; he had withstood the impact of Olympus without flinching, like Teneriffe or Atlas unremoved. But was I equal to the task? And was there not rather a danger that for the sake of peace and quietness I might be tempted to compromise, compound, and make terms? sinking thus, by successive lapses, into the Blameless Prig? I don't mean, of course, that I thought out my thoughts to the exact point here set down. In those fortunate days

of old one was free from the hard necessity of
transmuting the vague idea into the mechanical
inadequate medium of words. But the feeling
was there, that I might not possess the qualities
of character for so delicate a position.

The unnatural halo round Edward got more
pronounced, his own demeanour more re-
sponsible and dignified, with the arrival of his
new clothes. When his trunk and play-box
were sent in, the approaching cleavage between
our brother, who now belonged to the future,
and ourselves, still claimed by the past, was
accentuated indeed. His name was painted on
each of them, in large letters, and after their
arrival their owner used to disappear mysteri-
ously, and be found eventually wandering round
his luggage, murmuring to himself, 'Edward
———,' in a rapt remote sort of way. It was a
weakness, of course, and pointed to a soft spot
in his character; but those who can remember
the sensation of first seeing their names in print
will not think hardly of him.

As the short days sped by and the grim
event cast its shadow longer and longer across
our threshold, an unnatural politeness, a civility
scarce canny, began to pervade the air. In

those latter hours Edward himself was frequently heard to say 'Please,' and also 'Would you mind fetchin' that ball?' while Harold and I would sometimes actually find ourselves trying to anticipate his wishes. As for the girls, they simply grovelled. The Olympians, too, in their uncouth way, by gift of carnal delicacies and such-like indulgence, seemed anxious to demonstrate that they had hitherto misjudged this one of us. Altogether the situation grew strained and false, and I think a general relief was felt when the end came.

We all trooped down to the station, of course; it is only in later years that the farce of 'seeing people off' is seen in its true colours. Edward was the life and soul of the party; and if his gaiety struck one at times as being a trifle overdone, it was not a moment to be critical. As we tramped along, I promised him I would ask Farmer Larkin not to kill any more pigs till he came back for the holidays, and he said he would send me a proper catapult,—the real lethal article, not a kid's plaything. Then suddenly, when we were about half-way down, one of the girls fell a-snivelling.

The happy few who dare to laugh at the woes

of sea-sickness will perhaps remember how, on occasion, the sudden collapse of a fellow-voyager before their very eyes has caused them hastily to revise their self-confidence and resolve to walk more humbly for the future. Even so it was with Edward, who turned his head aside, feigning an interest in the landscape. It was but for a moment ; then he recollected the hat he was wearing—a hard bowler, the first of that sort he had ever owned. He took it off, examined it, and felt it over. Something about it seemed to give him strength, and he was a man once more.

At the station, Edward's first care was to dispose his boxes on the platform so that every one might see the labels and the lettering thereon. One did not go to school for the first time every day ! Then he read both sides of his ticket carefully ; shifted it to every one of his pockets in turn ; and finally fell to chinking of his money, to keep his courage up. We were all dry of conversation by this time, and could only stand round and stare in silence at the victim decked for the altar. And, as I looked at Edward, in new clothes of a manly cut, with a hard hat upon his head, a railway ticket in one pocket and money of his own in the other—money to spend as he liked and no questions asked!—I began to feel dimly how great was the gulf already yawning betwixt us. Fortunately I was not old enough to realise, further, that here on this little plat-form the old order lay at its last gasp, and that Edward might come back to us, but it would not be the Edward of yore, nor could things ever be the same again.

When the train steamed up at last, we all boarded it impetuously with the view of select-ing the one peerless carriage to which Edward might be intrusted with the greatest comfort and honour; and as each one found the ideal compartment at the same moment, and vocifer-ously maintained its merits, he stood some chance for a time of being left behind. A porter settled the matter by heaving him through the nearest door; and as the train moved off, Edward's head was thrust out of the window, wearing on it an unmistakable first-quality grin that he had been saving up somewhere for the supreme moment. Very small and white his face looked, on the long side of the retreating train. But the grin was visible, undeniable,

stoutly maintained ; till a curve swept him
from our sight, and he was borne away in the
dying rumble, out of our placid backwater, out
into the busy world of rubs and knocks and
competition, out into the New Life.

When a crab has lost a leg, his gait is still
more awkward than his wont, till Time and
healing Nature make him *totus teres atque
rotundus* once more. We straggled back from
the station disjointedly ; Harold, who was very
silent, sticking close to me, his last slender
prop, while the girls in front, their heads
together, were already reckoning up the
weeks to the holidays. Home at last, Harold
suggested one or two occupations of a spicy
and contraband flavour, but though we did
our manful best there was no knocking any
interest out of them. Then I suggested others,
with the same want of success. Finally we
found ourselves sitting silent on an upturned
wheelbarrow, our chins on our fists, staring
haggardly into the raw new conditions of our
changed life, the ruins of a past behind our
backs.

And all the while Selina and Charlotte were
busy stuffing Edward's rabbits with unwonted

forage, bilious and green ; polishing up the cage
of his mice till the occupants raved and swore
like householders in spring-time ; and collecting
materials for new bows and arrows, whips, boats,
guns, and four - in - hand harness, against the
return of Ulysses. Little did they dream that
the hero, once back from Troy and all its onsets,
would scornfully condemn their clumsy but
laborious armoury as rot and humbug and
only fit for kids! This, with many another
like awakening, was mercifully hidden from
them. Could the veil have been lifted, and the
girls permitted to see Edward as he would
appear a short three months hence, ragged
of attire and lawless of tongue, a scorner of
tradition and an adept in strange new physical
tortures, one who would in the same half-hour
dismember a doll and shatter a hallowed belief,
—in fine, a sort of swaggering Captain, fresh
from the Spanish Main,—could they have had
the least hint of this, well, then perhaps——.
But which of us is of mental fibre to stand the
test of a glimpse into futurity? Let us only
hope that, even with certain disillusionment
ahead, the girls would have acted precisely
as they did.

And perhaps we have reason to be very grateful that, both as children and long afterwards, we are never allowed to guess how the absorbing pursuit of the moment will appear not only to others but to ourselves, a very short time hence. So we pass, with a gusto and a heartiness that to an onlooker would seem almost pathetic, from one droll devotion to another misshapen passion; and who shall dare to play Rhadamanthus, to appraise the record, and to decide how much of it is solid achievement, and how much the merest child's play?

THE END

DISTRIBUTORS
for Wordsworth Children's Classics

AUSTRALIA, BRUNEI & MALAYSIA

Reed Editions
22 Salmon Street
Port Melbourne
Vic 3207
Australia
Tel: (03) 646 6716
Fax: (03) 646 6925

GERMANY, AUSTRIA & SWITZERLAND

Swan Buch-Marketing GmbH
Goldscheuerstraße 16
D-7640 Kehl am Rhein
Germany

GREAT BRITAIN & IRELAND

Wordsworth Editions Ltd
Cumberland House
Crib Street
Ware
Hertfordshire SG12 9ET

INDIA

Om Book Service
1690 First Floor
Nai Sarak, Delhi - 110006
Tel: 3279823/3265303
Fax: 3278091

NEW ZEALAND

Whitcoulls Limited
Private Bag 92098, Auckland

SINGAPORE

Book Station
18 Leo Drive
Singapore
Tel: 4511998
Fax: 4529188

SOUTHERN AFRICA

Struik Book Distributors (Pty) Ltd
Graph Avenue
Montague Gardens
7441
P O Box 193
Maitland
7405
South Africa
Tel: (021) 551-5900
Fax: (021) 551-1124

USA, CANADA & MEXICO

Universal Sales & Marketing
230 Fifth Avenue
Suite 1212
New York, NY 10001 USA
Tel: 212-481-3500
Fax: 212-481-3534

ITALY

Magis Books
Piazza della Vittoria 1/C
42100 Reggio Emilia
Tel: 0522-452303
Fax: 0522-452845